BRIGITTE BAUTISTA

You, Me, U.S.

First edition

Editing by Ronald Lim
Cover art by Dani Hernandez
Proofreading by Rica Forto

This book was professionally typeset on Reedsy.
Find out more at reedsy.com

To my cats Jeter and Blanchett,
for burying typos in my manuscripts,
and most importantly,
for saving my life.

Preface

Content Warning : This story contains references to domestic abuse and mild violence.

Chapter 1

S undays are for rest.

The hard deadline of hard work was Saturday night, and even that was pushing it. There was sanctity to weekends, Sundays even more so. Even God needed a break from Himself, from the never-ending cycle of creation and calamity. He deserved a day of leaving the salvation of the world up in the air. To Jo, Sunday was a respite, an escape, where she could go without caring if she was hungry, homeless, or broke. There was Monday for things like that. Sunday was for enjoyment.

And enjoy, she did. She enjoyed the white light filtering through the blinds. White. Not the dull, dusty yellow of her apartment. Not the seedy, eye-sore red of motels, reflected and refracted by those tacky ceiling mirrors. It was white, as God intended. She ran a hand across the sheets. They were warm and soft, not threadbare and gray from all the washing. She took her time rolling out of bed, her lover's bed, and allowed a swell of satisfaction to warm her stomach. The husband's car wasn't in the driveway, hadn't been there since yesterday. Light and nimble fingers pressed against Jo's ribs, gently pulling her back. Jo could just pick up her black Eraserheads crop top with one foot before falling back into her.

"Good morning," her lover mumbled, smelling of sleep and

pillows. "Make me breakfast, dear?"

A lazy day like this, Jo was tempted to give in. But she had been through too many mornings after. It was easy to predict how this would end. Lazy days like this, breakfast turned into lunch into dinner in a blur. Monday would announce itself with the crunch of gravel on the spacious driveway. She'd be jumping out of the balcony, acid-wash jeans between her knees. She'd be scampering with a broken ankle towards safety.

Despite the risks, Jo kept seeing the mistress because she liked her. She called her mistress, not in the context of infidelity, but as a term of endearment. Submissiveness, when the mood called for it. Her beauty was restrained, high-brow, prim and proper, not a single thing out of place. Jo usually had little patience for the filthy rich, but the mistress was the exception. There were signs that she could have been a wild child once. There could have been a time she didn't care about white blazers, wine and cheese pairings, and tiny snags on leather couches. Remnants of a free spirit still flickered in her eyes. A tiny tattoo, a cat under an umbrella, hid like a treasure under her breast. Though she rarely smiled now, her crow's feet told of years when she'd smiled wide and often.

The mistress could settle two months' rent easy. But Jo didn't let her pay. She didn't like to be kept and she hated getting paid on a Sunday. *It's a Sunday*, Jo would always tell her. *I don't work on Sundays.* Not that it stopped the mistress from insisting. The mistress liked her, cared for her even. But whatever she felt for Jo, there was no way in hell she would leave her husband. She couldn't part with this tortuous dullness, with never having to want anything. So weekends were a dead end for them, a loop they would keep on circling until one of them quit the ride. There was no illusion of taking it further, and they were both

2

fine with that.

"I don't do breakfasts. You know that."

"Wouldn't hurt asking."

"For the hundredth time?"

The mistress shrugged and smiled, twirling a finger around the hem of Jo's shirt. "How about a parting gift, instead?"

They had no rules on gifts in kind.

Jo made it home in the late afternoon. She passed by her landlady's unit to pay for rent, and for not asking questions whenever Jo got off a gray Mercedes C-class in front of the gate. She found Liza leaning against her door, stuffed backpack at her feet. She looked neat, like she was about to clock into her work shift at the department store, from the tight ponytail to the light makeup to the crease-free polo shirt and jeans.

Liza, Jo's best friend, hated the mistress. The mere mention of her name made Liza's blood boil. She couldn't understand how Jo could allow herself to be used like that. She kept telling Jo that she was being used, and there's no way she could come out of this on top. One time over lunch, Jo had answered that she came on top a record eight times. Liza choked on her water and left Jo to pay for the bill.

Liza heaved a sigh when she saw Jo, seemingly relieved. Not the response Jo expected, what with her crumpled clothes, wild wavy hair parted on one side. She waited for another hyperbole-ridden, mistress-directed sermon to start. But what was this now? No homily? Strange, as strange as the two balikbayan boxes beside her friend.

"Where have you been?" Liza said, checking her watch.

"To visit the queen. It's a Sunday, remember?" The sour look on Liza's face had Jo stifling a laugh. "You carried all that up here?"

"Yes, I did all the lifting." Sweat trickled down Liza's forehead. She immediately wiped it with a checkered hanky from her back pocket.

"Color me surprised." Jo clicked her tongue and pointed at the boxes. "What's the deal?"

"Endo."

"I thought you had that dorm deal locked in."

"It was supposed to be me and Sam. Split between us, the rent would still have been cheap. But the little nut just up and left. Drove that clunky car of hers and disappeared. With Ivy and Diane gone, I can't afford the whole space on my own."

"She'd rather hit the road than be stuck with you. That, I get," Jo said, testing if Liza would fire back. No petty jab or cheap shot came. Liza holding her tongue was as rare as snow in Manila. How bad was this endo?

"Can I stay here for a while?"

"Like you have to ask."

"I'd understand if you don't want to."

"Spare me the drama. Just get inside."

Relief and joy plain on her face, Liza grabbed Jo's cheeks and gave each one a grateful kiss. She mouthed a litany of *thank you, thank you, thank you, you're the best*, like a broken record. With a scowl, Jo quickly rubbed her face to get rid of the faint taste of sweat and cigarettes Liza left on her. She picked up one of the boxes and felt her arms buckle under the weight.

"What's in here, Liza? A body? Fuck, I will ride with you through hell and back, but no way I'll cover up a murder for you."

Liza turned to take the box herself. "Kojic and gluta soaps."

"Planning to be white as a ghost?"

"They're for selling, silly. To tide me over."

4

This wasn't Liza's first sleepover at Jo's. Endos brought Liza here from time to time. In Liza's line of work, an endo was a way of life. Jo was happy to share her small studio apartment until Liza got settled into a new six-month job. Breakups brought Liza here, too. That double-deck bunk bed Jo had thrown out last week had stains of Liza's lovelife grief all over it. There were times when Liza would come over just because, bearing closing-hour bread or chicken or some food she'd scored at the mall; Jo loved those sleepovers the most.

After a ten-minute water break, Jo cleared closet space for Liza's stuff before making early dinner. All she had was breakfast fare. She reached for the pack of dried fish in the cupboard, pulled out three tomatoes and a couple of eggs from the ref. She made rice good for three. Liza soon came hovering about, lured into the kitchen by the aroma of dried fish and garlic. Jo had a feeling this was going to be Liza's first meal since yesterday.

"Granted it's almost six p.m. But I thought you don't do breakfast."

"Don't flatter yourself. Sex marathons make me hungry."

Jo asked Liza to set the plates, while she attended to the kettle. She poured hot water into two cups and made black coffee. Equal parts sugar and cream for Liza. Straight-up, kick-you-in-the-gut black for Jo. A good ten minutes passed by without a word between them. Only slurps and the clink of spoon against plate stood in place of conversation. Silence had always made Jo uncomfortable, so she broke the ice first.

"So, how's Christopher?"

If the mistress was the villain extraordinaire in Liza's universe, then Christopher was Superman. He was the hero of all heroes. The sound of his name was enough to brighten the darkest of days. Liza smiled like there was no endo trouble to deal with. She chewed quickly so she could talk. Her hands gained a life of their own, flailing in animation at every Christopher anecdote.

Jo didn't like Christopher very much. Matter of fact, she didn't like any of Liza's deadbeat boyfriends. The men she'd dated in the past, all green-card holders, were total failures. Jo saw Liza through every single relationship. An endless string of flings and one near-miss.

"Doing okay. He's taken an interest in wood sculpture. Want to see his body—"

"Liza, oh my god, I'm still eating here."

"Body of work, I meant," Liza said, showing Jo a photo of a birdhouse. "You and your gutter mind."

Once Liza got started on Christopher, it would take a freight train hurtling through her to make her stop. Even though Jo would rather have her teeth pulled out with pliers than listen to this boring Christopher talk, she had to concede that Christopher distracted Liza from her endo troubles. Jo forced herself to smile and fake interest at birdhouses, lawn chairs, and coffee tables. Stuff she would never have to buy, thank heavens. *Look, here's Christopher's yard. Here's the inflatable pool in Christopher's yard. Here's Christopher soaking half-naked in the inflatable pool in Christopher's yard.* By the end of the slideshow, Jo knew Christopher's backyard like the lines on her palm.

Liza put down her phone and clasped her hands together, her eyes squinting. Jo knew what came next.

"Oh, Jo. I do hope he's the one."

There it was. *The One.*

Jo stuffed down a biting remark with a mouthful of rice. She twitched her eyeballs to stop them from throwing a snide side

6

eye. *Endo*, Jo reminded herself, *endo endo endo.* There was no use whipping a girl when she was down unless, of course, it was in the spirit of fulfilling a fetish, and that was another thing altogether. *He's the one. He's the one.* Jo had been through all fourteen The Ones. All the knockout-drunk, late-night, where-the-hell-am-I episodes because The One turned out to be just another one.

He's the one.

Why should she start believing now?

Jo sipped the rest of her coffee and said nothing.

Small as it was, Jo's apartment wasn't exactly a shining example of tidiness. Not that the mistress would ever sleep over here. She would probably freak out at how tiny Jo's studio apartment was. She would make a polite comment about how everything was within reach. Nevertheless, Jo changed the sheets. She cleaned up forgotten corners, wiped the sticky floor, and even arranged the bars of soap inside the closet. The little tasks added up to one exhausting evening, forcing them to call it quits by nine p.m.

"Take the right side," Jo offered. "The left is a bit creaky. And the sunlight burns your face in the morning from here."

Liza lay on the bed, messing up the sheets by rolling around like a little kid. She hit Jo, who was sitting on the edge, and wrapped her arms around her waist. "This new bed feels so good, Jo."

"Business is booming, what can I say?"

"I kinda miss the double deck, though. The memories."

"Yeah, the bed bugs, too."

They settled into the bed, making catch-up conversation while their thumbs scrolled up and down their phone screens. Liza checked in on her family in the province. She talked to her mother about the endo. Jo could tell whom Liza was talking to, just by the tone of her voice.

"I'll figure it out. Don't worry about it." Soft, reassuring, kind. This was *Aling* Luz. "Fingers crossed, not for long."

"Yes, baby?" Liza cooed, her lips puckering up like a duck. After a little more baby talk, her mouth curved into a smile. Mac, the youngest of the three Dimaandal siblings. "Yes, I'll get you that new bike if you promise to help *Nanay* with the chores."

"How much is your tuition again? Don't lie to me. Yes, you did that last time, if you need reminding." Sharp curses muttered under the breath, stern like that librarian Jo serviced once. This was Alex, the wayward brother with a bad case of middle-child syndrome.

"I just sent you five hundred last week. What do you mean, it's all gone?" Shrill, trying to be polite but failing miserably at it. Moans of frustration. *Mang* Carding probably wasted a good chunk of his allowance at mah jong. Or the cockpit. Or on one too many bottles of Emperador.

Liza hung up and, despite her troubled mind, soon fell asleep. Jo wasn't as lucky. She lay awake, hearing Liza mumble numbers in her dreams—or were those nightmares? She was probably running through the department stores and hyper-markets to apply to. Computing how much she should save per month for Alex's tuition. Dreaming of things Christopher could do with all that wood in his backyard.

Jo crept to the kitchen to fix herself a glass of milk. That and one last smoke ought to do the trick. She gazed at Liza, straddling a pillow with tense arms. Her brows were furrowed, the peace that slumber brought was lost on her. Jo wished she could carry some of the burden herself. But this was the best she could do. At least, a roof over Liza's head was one less thing to worry about. Jo slowly moved to the other side of the bed, the creaky and usually uninhabited half, and pulled the blanket up to Liza's waist. Jo hummed bits and pieces of a lullaby her mother used to sing to her, one that used to ward off the nightmares and let in the good dreams.

Chapter 2

As far as best friends went, Jo and Liza made quite the strange pair. Liza always seemed to be in a perpetual state of worry, always deep in thought, always trying to be a step ahead. A stark contrast to Jo's fly-by-your-pants, one-day-at-a-time approach to life. Liza was way better with money than Jo could ever be. Liza always knew exactly where each peso went. Jo, on the other hand, would book an ad, pay for the bills, and let the rest go like a flock of birds in the sun.

Liza grew up with the spoils of an OFW dad. Her father justified his absence by showering Liza with gifts. New toys, chocolates, and dresses that no other kid in their little town had. Sure, the other children had their fathers all the time. Their dads were home for dinner, after a day out fishing in the lake or tilling the fields. But they didn't have the towering doll house. They didn't have the Barbie party of five crammed inside a pink convertible. Their shelves didn't stock packets upon packets of chocolate that Liza ate until her tongue knew no other taste.

But the taste of the good life stopped when she was ten. Her father came home for good, after being discharged from his construction worker duties in Riyadh. He fell victim to a friend's misstep, a steel beam falling smack on him, pinning his arm dead. They said he was lucky it missed his head. Even then, they had to declare him incompetent. He went home that year without a new addition to Liza's Barbie collection. No chocolates to scatter from house to house. No face to show at church. For months, he was scared to go outside. He was fearful of the pitying stares. The hushed he-had-it-coming conversations behind his back scared him.

He recovered from the trauma, but never worked again. He milked his accident for all its worth. He had risked his own life and limb to give his family a good life. How much of a task was it for them to return the favor? He felt entitled to Liza's and Aling Luz's hard work. It was their turn to give him his dues. If he so much as washed a plate or fixed a lightbulb, he would badger Liza for gambling money. He rarely won the money back, but was good at promising to return it to Liza threefold. He never paid her back. Instead, he paid Liza and her mother with guilt every chance he got. That guilt kept Mang Carding alive. That guilt kept their humble fish-and-seafood stall afloat through good and bad. That guilt kept her brothers, Alex and Mac, in school.

As she grew up, Liza watched some of her neighbors leave for the U.S. She saw their lowly bungalows sprawl into three-story mansions. She watched her friends enjoy the very luxuries Mang Carding used to spoil her with. Liza convinced herself that living in the U.S. was the solution to their problems. She held on to that conviction and built a dream out of it. Annie, one of her childhood friends, became her partner in crime. She was a few years older than Liza, the resident mother hen to countless hours playing house. She, too, had dreams of busting out of their small lakeside town.

Despite their parents' disapproval, Liza and Annie dropped out of college and took a short vocational course on caregiving.

They ventured to Manila, both working as salesgirls, while they scoured the agencies for job vacancies.

***

"Promise me, we'll go together. And look out for each other," Liza said, while they exited the Redemptorist after the Wednesday novena.

"After everything we've been through, Liza, I wouldn't dare leave you."

"And, it's the U.S. or nothing."

"U.S. or nothing," Annie agreed, a quiver of reluctance in her voice.

In the end, only one of them kept her promise, while the other decided to apply to a post in secret. One of them landed a caregiver spot in Saudi, while the other was stuck in a salesgirl job in Manila. One of them was living their dream, while the other was in retail hell.

"Liza, please talk to me," Annie said when she called her the night before she left for Saudi. "I don't want to leave like this."

"You should have thought of that better when you hid that post from me."

"I needed the job."

"And, I didn't?"

They went back and forth, not getting anywhere near a reconciliation, until Annie gave up and considered their friendship over. For days, Liza lay ill in bed with a fever. She felt bitter about the betrayal, but was also envious of the future that lay ahead of Annie. On the third day, when the fever broke and she finally got herself out of bed, Liza vowed to do better. She swore it on her faded Piolo Pascual poster that she would live in the U.S. Unlike Annie, she would keep her promise.

***

The dream of someday living in the U.S. kept Liza going. It was the only way she could survive the hell of being a salesgirl. The hell of standing beside a shelf, barking out sales and promos, and looking pretty. As if anybody remembered their faces. As if anybody cared to spare more than a passing glance or even a half-hearted "Thank you."

Where to the Kids Section, miss? Take a right then go straight. Forgotten.

Do you have a size 13 for this? 4569A, 4569A, 13, please.

This doesn't fit, miss. This isn't my color. Arms heavy and laden with clothes turned inside out.

Liza's dream got a head start during a hectic Sunday end-of-season sale, when a co-worker urged her to give online dating a shot. After a hurried lunch, they shuttled to the retouching area. It was a small room cramped with rows upon rows of vanity dressers of cheap aluminum. Mara, a cashier and a relentless gossip, told her about a cousin who went on this site called FlowerBrides. Said cousin got herself an American husband.

"My god, Liza, if that cousin of mine can catch a foreigner, we can do it, too!" Mara said with a sigh before putting on her lipstick. She tilted her cheeks to the light, making sure the blush looked nice and even. "We should give it a try, at least. I'm sure we deserve better than this six months, six months life! I can't stand these contractual jobs anymore!"

They met after work at Liza's small bedspace. Ever the gossip, Mara had run her mouth around the whole Ladies Section, enticing a few others to come along. Armed with three bags of Chippy, a family-size Coke, and their phones, they ventured into this new world of dating. They debated on whether to use their real names or make-believe ones. They scrolled through the most popular profiles. They argued over how they would set themselves apart. Should they wear neon? Should they keep it simple? They took photos of each other and wagered a bet on who would get the most suitors in a week.

The weekly get-togethers became their own version of after-work fun. A pop of color in their monotonous lives, an escape to a world where they could be anyone they wished. High-society girl with a string of pearls around her neck. Rebel without a cause in ripped jeans. Housewife material, with a list of heirloom recipes to brag about. They didn't bat an eyelash at pretending. How bad could it be if the other person was half a world away? But the novelty wore off after a few months. The attendance grew thinner by the week. Most of Liza's friends soon tired of finding themselves a proper American husband. Even Mara, who'd started this whole online dating business, married a barista and called it a life.

Everyone but Liza gave up on the dream.

***

Jo had met Liza on her last working day at a KTV bar. That was five years ago, but it might as well have been a different life altogether. Fresh off the boat from Leyte, she'd thought herself too good for a small, typhoon-prone fishing village off the Eastern coast. Most of her friends ran away to Manila to become lawyers and doctors and rich housewives and such. Meanwhile, Jo ran away to become a singer. It was a huge bonus that she was as far away as possible from her father, who in turn ran away from reality by way of gin. Whenever she felt like going back, a keloid scar at the bottom of her armpit reminded her to stay put. In one of his episodes of drunken rage, her father had speared her with a fillet knife.

Looking at her now, no one would believe Jo once had dreams of becoming a pop star. She was a fresh-faced teen back then, brimming with confidence, ready to take a bite of the world. She thought herself a natural. She had been singing at every fiesta, birthday, wedding, and funeral since she was eight. She thought she was born for the fame and fortune of show business. She thought success was as easy as barging into the big studios and belting one out. She thought that fame was written in her palms. She believed it like the certainty of tides and sunsets. She had the pipes for it, and she fancied herself the next Sarah Geronimo. If not that, then she'd settle for Angeline Quinto. Worst case, she'd bend backwards for a one-off single like those tone-deaf matinee TV idols. If they could do it, her inner ear should fare way better. But with Dion or Houston or Aegis, she didn't make the cut at any one of those auditions. Even when she had circled through all the power ballads she knew, the rejections kept piling up. The money she stole from her parents wasted away. Soon, all she had left was a pair of pretty dresses and a stack of 3R headshots.

Jo found out the hard way that chasing your dreams was a lie. The best you could do was make them smaller and smaller until they came true. Struggling to fund her auditions and pay for rent, she decided to set her sights lower. She gave up on the TV competitions. She stopped bothering with mall shows as well. Her pop star dreams weren't filling her stomach or paying the bills. So she shrunk them until they were nothing but a dot. Insignificant. Nothing of substance, consequence, or importance.

In this state of despair, she found a vacancy sign on one of the KTV bars she passed along her way home. *Pleasing personality. Good voice. Attractive face. Inquire inside.* She fit two out of three. Her personality needed work, but nothing a little acting won't fix. She clung to it as her own sign of salvation and signed herself up for the job. In that tiny KTV bar, Jo could not be farther away from stardom.

At least, she got the singing part all right. She sang every night for eight hours, sometimes twelve, changing tables and partners on the hour. Applause was welcome. But most of the time, they wolf-whistled and called her sweet tits or pussy or asked, how about a blow job. She got paid a little extra if she agreed to a little groping, or if she got sent to the VIP room, or if a customer took her out. But considering how much Mama-san got out of each transaction, the nightly bonus was far from a fair deal. Many things about her job pissed her off. One time, she got pissed at missing a note because she was straddling a soon-to-be-married man. The red lights pissed her off, too, and made her right eye permanently hazy. The clients had to keep drinking, so she had to keep drinking. Drinking reminded her of her father, and that didn't sit well with her at all.

But the thing that angered Jo the most was surrendering her freedom. She gave up her right to an opinion and choice, all for what? Free food and a room upstairs? She didn't mind selling pleasure as a service. There was nothing wrong with adults doing adult things on a Friday night. What she minded was not having control over who she got to do adult things with. Sure, only adults could enter the KTV bar. But Jo soon learned that some adults were bigger assholes than others. Every night, Mama-san sent marching orders to a table. Every night, Jo was left to trust her horrible luck that she didn't get the drunken uncles or the police.

That one night, though, she did get the police. Matter of fact, all the girls did. These weren't the usual fare of city police, those blue shirts with oversize pants and bellies to boot. The blue shirts kept the bar a secret in exchange for a couple of VIP passes. That night, the real police showed up. Black caps and black shirts and trim waists. Jo remembered that night, couldn't forget no matter how she tried. It was like a hot summer day that turned to rain and had everyone running for shelter. Waitresses ran around, covering their faces with aprons and itty-bitty scarves. The mama's boys scurried out of the bar or hid under tables. Jo had drawn the VIP room that night. She was in the middle of a hand job when the commotion started downstairs. She peered through the cracks in the door and found Mama-san outside her office. There was a policeman with her. Jo knew she had to run and take cover like the others, but panic had taken over her limbs. It was the shattering of a beer bottle that got her back to her senses. She waited for Mama-san and the head of police to convene in the next room. Once clear, she hurried downstairs and slipped through the kitchen. She crouched down and duck-walked to a backdoor for deliveries and smoke breaks. She made a mad dash to the exit just as a policeman said, "Oy!"

The chase was on.

Jo knew there was no way to outrun them. So, armed with a smirk and a mental map, she turned every corner and alley if only to make it interesting. In jail, Jo could brag about how she had the MPD running around their own turf like headless chickens. They should leave her alone after that, or make her a gang boss. She'd have her choice of prison wives, how about that? The two policemen spotted her when she stopped to lean and rest against a wall of peeled-away campaign posters. Her feet were swollen, legs aching at the joints. She made no attempt to move; she even had her hands up as high as her strength allowed. The chase was over. This was the end of her dreams. In a way, Jo was relieved.

"Hey, cousin! Been looking all over for you. Did you get lost?"

A woman Jo had never met was waving at her from across the street. She walked towards Jo and beat the two police blokes to it. She gripped Jo by the arm and pushed her past the sidewalk vendors.

"I told you it's Bonifacio Street. Not J. Luna, silly. And what are you all dressed up for? It's just a simple party!"

"Excuse me, ma'am. Do you know this woman?" The policeman tapped the stranger on the shoulder.

Jo and the woman looked at each other. While Jo's eyes held defeat, the woman gave her a wink and a half-smile. *Play cool. Just go with it. See what happens,* she seemed to say. The smile was gone when she turned around to face the policemen, her lips transformed into a thin line.

"Yes," the stranger said with a nod.

"I'm sorry but we need to arrest her."

"An arrest? For what?"

"For prostitution." The words barely came out of the policeman's mouth when a ringing slap hit him on the face. His partner was shocked—so was Jo. The sidewalk vendors, who had tuned into the police drama, gasped in almost-unison. Hell, even the moon looked quite shaken.

"Are you calling my cousin a whore?" the woman screamed, loud enough for the whole of J. Luna to hear.

Jo saw the policeman take a deep breath, his nostrils flaring from the effort. This chase was probably more than what his pay grade justified. "Really, ma'am. We have no time for this. If you could please surrender her to us."

"What proof do you have?"

"Well, we were chasing a girl that matches her description."

"And, what description is that?"

"Tall, thin, brown hair, red dress."

"Why, anyone could be tall, thin, brown hair, in a red dress! What makes you so sure you're not wrong?" The woman argued, hands on her hips, standing firm in front of Jo.

"Ma'am, she had her hands raised in surrender."

The woman raised her arms and waved them in mockery. "Going to arrest me now, are you?"

"If you could please surrender her to us, ma'am, and we'll be on our way."

"Fuck, no. She's my cousin!"

After a heated exchange, the policemen grew tired of arguing. It was already late in the night. They had already wrangled in twenty others, including the head of the beast. What was letting one loose? The woman, this unlikely savior, didn't stop running her mouth until the policemen were well out of sight.

Slack-jawed in disbelief, Jo followed the woman to a nearby bedspace. She'd been so sure she would rot in a jail cell. But here she was, warming her hands with a cup of coffee. She wasn't down on the floor on all fours, suffering from a strip search. Instead, she was sitting upright on a weathered Monobloc stool, with all her clothes on her. A wall fan blew cool air on her face.

"So sorry I had to call you a whore back there," the woman said, extending a packet of Marlboros instead of a handshake. "It's Liza, by the way."

"Jo." Jo took a cigarette from Liza's packet. Her hands were still trembling. If it was due to the hand job from earlier or the threat of jail time, she couldn't tell for sure. "And, thank you. I guess this is the part where I say I owe you my life."

Liza dismissed the gratitude with a wave of her hand. "People here have it hard enough to have the police on their ass, too. And, besides—Jo, did I hear that right?—that pretty voice has no place in prison."

"You heard me sing?"

"A couple of times," Liza said, waving two fingers in the air. "Janice, you know Janice, I bet. Blonde, short-ish, obsessed with red lipstick? I supply her imported makeup at a discount. The first time I made a delivery, I waited at a table out back. Creepy old place. Had to keep telling the customers that I didn't work there. Wanted to forget the deal and get out of there. But I heard you sing and it was... suddenly, it wasn't all that bad."

A faint blush crept to Liza's cheeks. "OK, fine. I have a little crush on you, I guess."

Awful at taking compliments, Jo rubbed the back of her neck, clicked her tongue, and looked away. The silence unsettled her, while she waited for Liza to speak again. Thank heavens she didn't have to wait for very long.

"What are you going to do now?"

"I don't know. The bar will be shut down for some time, I'm sure. So, I don't know, something else? I'll think of something. But, really, thank you." Jo had to repay this gesture somehow. She leaned closer and placed her hand on Liza's thigh, right above the knee. "Is there any way I can make it up to you? Fix you up?"

Liza leaned closer, so close Jo could see the slight curve of her eyelashes. Looking Jo in the eye, Liza plucked Jo's hand from her thigh and restored the space between them. Jo's stomach tightened at the rejection. She flirted a lot, on the job and off it, and rarely missed.

"If I need something, I'll let you know," Liza said. With a chuckle and a shake of the head, she walked to the sink and got a glass of water. "Get some rest. Don't make me regret saving your ass."

That chance meeting became the start of a strong friendship, a rare occurrence in Jo's life. She found it hard to connect with people; no, not in that one-time-thing kind of way, but in that deeper ride-or-die, go-to-hell-with-you kind of way. She took Liza's words to heart, and never gave her reason for regret. Although she refused Liza's persistent urging to hook her up with a foreigner boyfriend, she was there through all the breakups.

The first of Liza's exes that Jo witnessed was Brian, a thirty-year-old surfer dude from California. This breakup was tame and over quickly. Rated on the pain scale, it was barely a 2. Brian had abs and biceps for days, and Liza practically went in heat every time he sent a new photo. Jo even joked about pursuing him herself. All was good until Brian confessed that he had never surfed a day in his life. He was, in fact, eighty years old and living out his days in a retirement home. Chatting up young women half a world away was his daily recreation, completely oblivious of how seriously Liza took this online dating business. Of how she staked her life and future on every relationship.

They sat outside Liza's bedspace after the breakup, staking a spot by the narrow sidewalk, a small tub of ice cream sitting on its own Monobloc between them. Between mouthfuls of Double Dutch ice cream, Liza told Jo about how Brian proposed to her.

"OK, so he asked if we could chat on video. He never does that, you know! I thought we were stepping it up. Out of the getting-to-know phase, finally! Face to face! Naturally, I agreed and even asked for time to put a pretty dress on." Liza sighed and pinched the bridge of her nose. She returned a snort from Jo with a mean glare. "The screen came on and he was..."

"A raisin?"

"Don't be mean to elders, Jo." Liza slapped Jo's arm. "And, then, he asked me to marry him."

"He what?" Jo said, cheeks puffy from keeping the laughter in. "Tell me you said no."

"Of course I said no! He was three coughs away from death!"

"Wow! And I'm mean?"

Liza bit her lower lip until she couldn't hold it any longer. She burst out laughing, that scandalous, devil-may-care laugh that Jo absolutely loved. Strangers stared. Tricycle drivers slowed down. Even a stray dog stopped to cock its head at them.

"An eighty-year-old ex. I don't think I've had that one yet. You win this one, Liza." Jo pretended to pick a tiara from a pretend-table and put it on Liza's head.

"It's not funny. Now, I'm back to zero."

"Oh, Liza, come on. Take it easy. He won't be your last, okay? You're cute and quite the talker and you make a really mean adobo."

"Is that a compliment you're voluntarily giving me?"

Jo rolled her eyes and shifted her gaze to the moonless sky. "I mean, there's a horde of people out there who's into boxy starched dresses. I'm sure you're going to fulfill a very specific need."

"Bitch."

Jo stuck her tongue out before flashing Liza a toothy grin. "I'm your bitch."

***

The next series of breakups were uneventful. Either they were amicable or Liza was getting used to the drama. Jo had her reservations about Liza's online partners, but none—at least, until the last one—riled her up except Marcus the Zombie. This one didn't like sleeping very much. While most of Liza's suitors called at night, Marcus called almost every hour of every day. He would call Liza during lunch. He was always there, in all his

22

pixelated glory, when she retouched her makeup in the middle of her shift. He would be ready for a video call when Liza got home. He kept her up until four in the morning.

Jo was walking home from her shift at the laundromat when she received an emergency call about Liza.

"Hello. Ms. Joanna Suarez?"

"Yes. Who is this?"

"I'm Dr. Palma. Liza Dimaandal, one of our employees, listed you as an emergency contact."

"What happened? Is she okay?"

"She's resting right now. I've given her an analgesic for the headache. She collapsed on the floor during her shift. Granted, the mall was packed because of the three-day sale. This heat could also be a factor. But I do think it's sleep deprivation. Would you know if she has been sleeping well?"

Marcus.

"Can you come pick her up?"

Bone-tired and sleepy herself, all Jo wanted was to lie in bed and rest for the next day. Instead, she hailed a jeep to the opposite direction, towards the mall. She picked up Liza, still woozy from her nap, her unusual silence an apology in itself. Jo didn't say a word all throughout the ride home—from the stopover at the drugstore, to a quick dinner at Mang Larry's, to the walk along Liza's street.

"Are you mad?"

Jo took a long drag of her cigarette. She wanted to blow all this smoke at Liza's face. But at the sight of Liza's glassy eyes and pursed lips and hunched shoulders, she decided against it. "It's your life. If you want to drop dead surrounded by cheap-ass shoes and become an actual zombie, that's on you."

Liza poked at Jo's ribs. "Come on, Jo. The truth?"

"Am I mad?" Jo scoffed. "Of course, I am! You think it's fun getting a call that your best and only friend, the only one you care about anyway, just collapsed in the middle of a shift? You think it's fun telling you time and time again to quit this guy, and have you go all 'Oh, but he's so nice and cute' because he has a well-groomed beard? You think working with two hours of sleep is some feat you can be proud of? Well, congratulations, you win two weeks of unpaid leave!"

Liza responded with a tight embrace. Jo wanted to wriggle out of it, but felt her anger slowly subsiding.

"Jesus, Liza. Don't make me worry like that. What would I tell Aling Luz if something worse happened to you?"

Liza broke off the embrace to fish out her ringing phone. Of course, Marcus. 24/7 Marcus. Liza looked at Jo, let out a sigh, and canceled the call. Instead, she typed away before showing the screen to Jo.

Marcus, I'm breaking up with you.

"Thank you, Jo."

"Enjoy your Gatorade. I made sure I bought three of the blue ones. I know you like that shit," Jo said as a goodbye, shoving the plastic bag of multi-colored sports drinks in the space between them.

***

They enjoyed another ceasefire of bad breakups until the fourteenth one came along. Oh, the fourteenth, he did Liza good. They couldn't even say his name now; that's how bad he was. If the others joined forces and became a person, they wouldn't even be half as awful as this guy. He looked decent. He had a good job. He didn't lie about being forty. He let Liza have her sleep. He had Liza thinking that all these years of online dating had finally paid off. He had Liza hoping she would get it right this time. He was the closest to an engagement Liza got. He talked about taking time off work, booking a trip, and meeting her parents. Then, he disappeared. He went offline, not only in the dating service but in all his social networks. Liza worried herself sick for weeks. What if something happened to him? Had he gotten killed or sick or thrown into jail? He came up for air eventually, parading his new Filipina wife.

"Come on, Liza. That's enough," Jo said, snatching the last bottle of Pale Pilsen from Liza's already-floppy grip. She looked at the time on the dirty wall clock. One a.m. "Up, up now. We have work in four hours."

"Just one more bucket."

"No, come on. Up, up, up."

Jo practically dragged Liza out of the bar and to her place, then a small six-square-meter hole. Liza hurled her regrets straight into the toilet bowl, no regret bigger than downing a whole bucket of beer by herself. Jo chuckled, while preparing two cups of coffee.

"Why would he do that? Why would he marry someone else and not tell me?" Liza said, wincing as she rubbed the side of her head.

Jo set down the coffee. Liza raised two unsteady fingers, one almost poking her in the eye. Jo scooped two tablespoons of sugar and cream into Liza's cup.

"You know what, I'm gonna call him," Liza slurred. "I'm gonna... I'm gonna. Yes, call him. Get the truth out of his mouth, that's what I'm gonna do. Call him. Yes. Yes. Don't stop me." Liza slapped the air, completely missing Jo's cheek. If she were aiming for it at all.

"I don't think that's a good—"

"Shhhhh."

25

"It's your funeral." Jo knew when to surrender, and allowed Liza to make the rare, ill-thought mistake. She watched amusedly as Liza squinted at her phone and pressed the screen repeatedly. Props to her. Punch-drunk and still able to call her ghosting boyfriend.

"Hoy! You! How dare you! Why would you do that to me? What did I do to deserve that?"

Silence. More tears. Finally, after what felt like an eternity of one-sided conversation, the phone, slippery with sweat and tears, was laid to rest on the table. The call seemed to have sobered up Liza.

"That's not a good look. What did he say?"

"His wife was younger. And cheaper to maintain."

That was that. Marriage was a matter of economics to him. Jo could only sigh and awkwardly place her hand on Liza's shoulder. She wasn't a fan of hugging at all. Liza clutched Jo's hand with her own, as they both braced for the aftermath of another heartbreak.

Chapter 3

W hile Liza cycled through her green-card prospects, Jo took on a carousel of odd jobs, trying to find one good enough to keep her comfortable—time-sharing a pedicab out and about Quinta Market, delivering laundry door to door, running a *saklaan* for fake wakes. Sometimes, it was one of these; most of the time, it was all of the above. The world of casual encounters opened to Jo quite by accident. She was looking for a bigger space than her six-square-meter hole, when she took a wrong click and fell into a rabbit hole of propositions for one-night stands and high-class escorts and girlfriends-for-hire. Two days of scrolling through the same ads over and over, Jo decided she'd try her luck on this freelance trade. She posted her best photos and drew a forgettable man for her first ad. He came with a three-inch penis she would also rather forget.

Her clients were a mixed bag but weren't usually so terrible. One out of ten, perhaps, she would get a freak out of nowhere. Like that ad with the foulest package ever. Decently endowed, sure. But up close and personal, you would think he washed his junk with Manila Bay water. The request sounded easy enough, just a couple of blow jobs. But when she got in there, it was like walking pitch dark into a sewer. She didn't gag easy—intestinal fortitude was a virtue she took pride in. But that time, she couldn't keep it in. Jo threw up all over him. Stomach. Thighs. Calves. All the fuck over. All she got paid with was the echo of her own laughter all the way home and a story to tell for years to come.

Even through the bad calls, being her own boss was strangely liberating. At the bar, Jo had everything else to blame but herself. Blame Mama-san for her ridiculous sense of work politics. Blame that girl on unpaid leave who got an infection : this should have been her table. Blame the tables. Blame the customers sitting at the tables. Blame your luck. On the surface, it was comforting to blame something else for your troubles. But at the root of it, if she couldn't blame herself, then she wasn't in control. She wasn't free to fuck up the way she chose to fuck up.

Through practice, she got better and better at choosing. The whole world wanted to get laid, and she soon realized that she had liberty of choice. As a rule, she avoided the generics, those boring one-and-done phone-sex types who wrote on the backs of bus seats all over Manila. They were only good for easy cash, when rent was due and Jo was all tapped out. She favored the outliers, those who had a kink or two up their sleeve, those who were either too specific or too vague. The too-specifics always have a shopping list of requests and requirements, like they were the experts. Jo let them run their mouth. *Come on, boy, explain to me how sex should be done.* But in the end, it was Jo who did the schooling. The too-vagues were cute, and were usually the shy types. The newbies were a treat from time to time, too. They would hint at what they wanted, skirt around, and pretend to know what they were talking about.

***

Tonight, Jo could tell her ad was a newbie. Her message was devoid of the online jargon that most of her regulars were already fluent in. No online slang like w4w, sop, bdsm. She even left Jo a nice little verse at the bottom of the message. *My imagination has reached its limit. I have tasted every word and phrase with my mind. Reality must kick in or I will be the worse for it.*

With that poem? Done deal. Besides, Jo was in the mood for a little mentoring. She passed on Cuddle Buddy and Just Curious and clicked on her young newbie poet.

"Hi."

"Is this safe?" the newbie responded. *See, already starting on the right foot with this one.*

"Yes."

"Will I go to jail?"

"Not if you don't drown me in the toilet bowl or strangle me with a towel."

"Are you clean? Or is that even the right term? Sorry if I don't say stuff right."

"I do regular checkups. Could show you medical clearance if you like."

"Will it hurt?"

Jo paused before writing, "Like a bitch."

The chat thread went silent. Jo was sure her half-joke had scared her away. She was already thinking of a response to Cuddle Buddy when her newbie poet responded with a time and place. Now that they were in the safe zone, Jo chatted her up a little bit more. Ad was an engineering student from the state university. Of legal age, by way of a voter's ID. The ad had straight-cut, flat hair, a button nose, thin lips that hardly moved when she smiled. Minimalistic.

They agreed to meet at a business hotel near the train station. For an unemployed twenty-year-old student, she spent better than most of Jo's clients. She confessed that she stole from Mommy to fund this experiment, insisting that she would pay back in secret installments. Mommy was always up her ass about her grades and classes. She had to make up a story about an evening class just so she could have a free night to herself. Sneaky. Clever. Jo was starting to like her.

"What kind of friends do you have?" Jo asked. The ad shook her head and looked away.

"Friendship is a pain, anyway. I only have one friend and there are days I want to quit on her," Jo said, an attempt at commiseration. "Any boy or girl who'd be pissed you're doing this?"

"Do you think I'd be with you if I had one?"

"Ouch," Jo said, rubbing her chest, pretending to be hurt.

While waiting for the elevator, the ad kept glancing at another couple. The ad didn't want to ride with them. So they waited for the couple to get going, and boarded the next available elevator. She asked Jo for the umpteenth time if this was OK.

"It's your show. Whatever you want." Jo paused to wiggle her index finger. "Except bondage. That will cost you extra."

"Do you like girls? Or guys? Or it's just money to you?"

"In order? Let me think." She liked girls more than the rest, but not by much. "If I had to line them up, I'd say girls. Then, boys six inches and up. Then, all the rest of them. I am a bit choosy, though. Even when I get paid."

"Do you like me?"

"You're not so bad. Could use a little makeup."

The ad drew a hand to her cheek, suddenly self-conscious, and started fishing for a compact in her leatherette bag. Jo chuckled and gave her hand a gentle slap.

"I'm kidding, I'm kidding. You look nice. Not in a movie star kind of way. But you look better than you think," Jo said, her laughter putting the ad momentarily at ease. She was, at least, comfortable enough to give in to a short scoff.

"You're not what I expected. You don't..."

"Kiss ass?" Jo asked.

"Bleed flattery."

"That was nice. Mind if I jack that phrase?" Jo said, chuckling again. "Bleed flattery."

The higher up they went, the faster the ad's fingers drummed against her thigh. Jo laced her fingers around the ad's wrist and gave her a wink. The ad took a deep breath as the elevator opened to their floor. The room was clean and no-nonsense, faithful to the whole business hotel vibe. A small table stood right beside the door, the bed a few steps inside. A pixelated photo of a seaside town rested above the headboard, a feeble attempt at sophistication. The ad sat on the edge of the bed, feet not quite planted on the carpet floor, as if ready to bolt any second. She ran her hand nervously through the sheets. She scrolled through her phone. She fixed her bag. Jo leaned on the cabinet and watched the ad with curiosity, waiting for her to run out of things to do. When she finally did, she looked up at Jo.

"So?"

Jo undressed her slowly, starting with the shoes. Gray Converse high-tops, with purple shoelaces.

"Do you really have to do that?"

This ad sure knew how to ask questions. Jo told her to be quiet, but in a gentle tone, not in that hissing tone when she wanted Liza to stop yakking about Christopher. Jo could hear her swallow as Jo unbuttoned her shirt. She trembled at the warmth of Jo's palm on her arm. Jo gave her space and held an unassuming stance, proceeding only upon her expressed approval. A nod. A verbal yes. A tentative tug. Jo let her kiss first. She let the ad say how fast or how slow. She let her roam where her curiosity led her. She let her say where, when, how. It took a while for the trembling to stop, but Jo appreciated the quiver of a smile on those minimalist lips. In the end, she came into it on her own, came on her own. Jo was just an invisible hand guiding things along.

They nested under the sheets, Jo's head resting on a double layer of pillows. The ad had been spread-eagled for a good two minutes. She was staring at the ceiling, taking in air by the lungful. There were muffled sounds from a room nearby. TV? Radio? Or maybe they were having a good time as well.

"So, how's reality?" Jo asked, referring to the Lang Leavesque snippet the ad posted online. The ad blushed and buried her face in her hands, sinking her head deeper into the pillow.

"You read that?"

"Course I did. It's why I clicked. I always appreciate A-plus word play. So, how is this for your first time?"

The ad sat up and sighed, her button nose crinkling up. "You won't get mad?"

"Why would I be?" Jo replied, although the power of suggestion had worked on her. She was feeling a bit annoyed already.

"Reality was good and all. But I feel like I'm missing a part of it. A huge part of it. Like, you're trying to breathe. You're drowning. Your body's going wild on you. Your eyes are closed and you're trying to bring that one person to mind. Pray for someone to make sense of all this. Just grab your hand and pull you out. And, my mind just stayed dark. It was good but, the moment after, it felt a little lame."

Lame was a trigger word. Jo hated hearing that about her work. "Do you want to try again?" she asked, straightening up at the prospect of a challenge.

They gave it another go. And another. And another. And another. They tried five times, like circling through a bunch of keys just to open one lock. Each of those five times, the ad gave in to the high, to the jerking, to the moans of pleasure. A moment of calm would pass between them; in that moment, she was happy and content. Then, the moment would pass, and she was more miserable than the last go-round.

"Still blank?" Jo asked. The ad gave a slight nod and curled up into her. She was such a good sport, it was hard to stay mad at her after a night of trial and error. "You know what, you remind me of my friend. Thinks sex is only for *The One*."

"Oh? And how did that go for her?"

"It's always *The One* with her. Although I think most of it is online, so that may not count. Well, who's to say what kind of sex counts and doesn't?"

"Is it so bad to wait for The One before I do this again?"

"Like I said, it's your body, sweetie. You can wait, not wait, do it once, do it always, do it never."

After a quick shower, they left the hotel and parted ways at the train station. Jo caught the last train home and found herself thinking about how frustrating the evening had been. It didn't add up. The ad had her licks and looked satisfied. But Jo didn't feel like she'd done a good job. Maybe, it was all that go-to person talk. Someone to go to in her head. What was she expecting to see? God? Jesus? Her parents? High school crush? Jo bounced the idea around until her own head ached from the effort.

Liza was still up when Jo got home. She found her sitting on the bed, face aglow with white light from her phone. Worrying about bills again, if the creased forehead and harsh frown were any indication. Jo offered her a bag of donuts. One was half-eaten. She got hungry doing some post-ad debriefing.

"Why are you still up?"

"Mac and Alex will be starting school soon. Plus, Mama called to say the last storm broke the window in the dirty kitchen. And, Papa—the usual."

"*Sabong,*" they said at the same time, referring to Mang Carding's habitual trips to the cockpit, before breaking into laughter.

They made coffee and convened by the window, a new habit they had picked up on. Jo took a cigarette. A gust of wind blew through, snuffing out the flickering flame of Liza's lighter. Liza lit it again, leaned closer and tucked Jo's hair away from the flame, sending a cold shiver coursing through Jo. Uncomfortable with the space, or rather lack thereof, Jo almost choked on a quick drag and shifted her head away.

"Hey, I may have found your long-lost, lovesick twin."

"Well, what did you tell her about me?"

"I may have told her you were into online sex."

That earned Jo a hard slap on the arm. Jo told her about the ad and how she made her come every single time and still left her feeling like a job half-done. She complained about the ad's insistence on searching for a go-to person, an image that would give her orgasms more meaning.

"I'm not heartless, Liza. Just because I don't get that lovey-dovey shit doesn't mean everyone should be me. She's twenty years old. She wants to be like you, be my guest. She wants to fall in love before her orgasms could make any sense, that's her wet dream. If I tell her what I think, it would be for me. Not for her. So, I sent her home. With a sampling of orgasms, let the record state that."

"Yes, you've made that fact clear as day. Want me to hang a medal around your neck?" Liza clapped in mockery. Jo responded with a half-bow and a curtsy. "You self-absorbed ass."

From the window, they watched the city transform. This time of night, the landscape took on a new life. The buildings and houses were mere shells, the substance inside them shifting as the day wore on. The grayed and yellowed morphed into hot white and neon. The darkness lurked, but only in its own small circles.

"Well, who do you think of?"

"I don't need to have someone in my mind to get off, thank you very much."

Liza put her mug down and looked at Jo. Her hand crept closer, brushing against Jo's fingers resting on the window ledge. Jo gave her a slight smile and took a big gulp of her coffee.

"Do you ever think of me?" Liza asked.

Out of nowhere, just like her question, a spray of coffee hit Liza straight in the face. Liza huffed as she cleaned it up with the collar of her shirt, while Jo coughed and hacked and wheezed her breathing back to normal.

"Guess that's a no."

Chapter 4

"**N**o way! Oh, my god! Don't joke about this, babe. Are you serious?" The tiny smile on Liza's face grew to a full-blown toothy grin. A slight blush crept to her ears. After almost half an hour, Liza finally hung up, the same ear-to-ear smile still plastered on her face.

"Christopher's coming to visit! He's coming to visit!" She jumped up and down like a little kid on a sugar rush, and started attacking the flesh on Jo's arms with small, painful pinches. "I'm going to see him at last!"

"Ouch," Jo said, slapping away Liza's fingers.

"This is perfect. I'm having drinks at the Appliance Center later. You want to come? Unless you have plans."

Liza's friends from her previous work were jacking the Appliance Center again. She got invited to an after-closing movie night. They did this sometimes. Plug a movie into the biggest TV on the floor and make a night out of it. It was a Saturday; Liza knew where Jo would be later. But for some reason, she wished Jo would cancel her plans and spend the night with her.

"No. Nothing planned. Why?"

"No mistress?" Liza said, prodding, curious.

"She's in some Batangas beach club with the husband. She did send me bikini photos. Wanna see?"

"I'm good. Thanks." Liza stopped Jo from scrolling through her gallery. "Pick you up later?"

"You live here, Liza. Don't make it sound like a date."

Driven by the promise of a good night out, Liza went about her day scouring the city for a job. She started out hopeful, positive this would be the day that would end her job-hunt losing streak. After another day of waiting in line at a recruitment agency, it seemed that the streak was indeed about to end. Her chances at a grocery store job post looked promising. Finally. She had been subsisting on Kojic soap sales for close to a month.

Pleased with herself, she walked to the nearest 7-Eleven and ordered herself a feast of half-cooked treats. Bola-bola. Hotdog sandwich. A bowl of hot pot. She reached for an ice-cold Coke from the back of the fridge. Her eyes widened when she recognized the woman behind the counter.

"Annie?"

For the longest time, Annie's reality had been the stuff of Liza's daydreams. While she had long forgiven Annie for breaking her promise, it still hurt thinking about the life she could have had if she had gotten the post. Through the years, Annie had managed to transform her family's shack in Laurel into a three-story house in pink and white. Last she heard, Annie had married a Saudi local and reared two toddlers of her own. She should be close to thirty or thirty-one now, but could easily be mistaken for a forty-year-old. A scar under the right eye broke her smooth complexion.

"What happened? Oh my god, why are you here? When did you come back? Where are your kids?" Liza didn't realize she was holding up the queue.

Annie wasn't quite ready for the ambush interrogation. "Liza? Liza Dimaandal?"

"Yes, it's me!" Liza smirked. "The one you betrayed, remember?"

Annie fell silent.

"Oh, come on. I was just kidding. We were young, then. All forgotten." Liza waved her hand, as if wiping their slate clean.

"Hey, uh, Liza, I'm on break in fifteen minutes. Maybe we could catch up then?"

Liza hung back outside until Annie could afford that break. As soon as Annie sat across from her, Liza resumed with the questions. They held hands, the joy of seeing a familiar face coursing through their tightly pressed palms. Annie's face reflected Liza's delight, but hers was also tinged with shame and regret.

"Good to see you and all, but what happened? I thought you had it made."

"I thought I had it, too, Liza."

"Did you lose your job? Did you get involved in something illegal? Was there an accident?" Liza remembered her OFW father and meeting him at the airport. She was excited then because her mother hadn't told her the truth that her father had been sacked and would be home for good.

Annie shook her head. A bitter smile played on her lips, marring an otherwise kind-looking face. "I wish I had lost my job. I wish I wasn't good at it. That would have been easier. Discharged from duty, that would be all right. That way, I didn't have to endure the beatings my husband gave me." By habit, her fingers traced the scar under her eye, the one Liza noticed earlier. She rolled her short sleeve to show Liza a set of circular scars. "Cigarette burns."

Liza winced. Her heart gave out a little lurch, as if she, too, were peppered with a half-spent stick of Marlboro. This wasn't what Liza expected at all. Sure, she once wished for Annie's failure. She once prayed Annie would encounter a misfortune so big they had to sell their big house and move back to a shack. But those were childish prayers, ill wishes spoken out of envy. Seeing her like this, scarred and bitter, did not give Liza any kind of satisfaction.

"The last straw was when he beat me with a frying pan. He didn't even have a drink in him. Didn't provoke him or anything, you know me." Annie traced the contour of her hairline with slightly trembling fingers. "He did it to show he could. My sons were watching, and that's when I knew I had to get out of there. I asked Mama if we could sell the house so I could go home. I sought help from all the Pinoys I knew. Fellow caregivers. The embassy even. Luckily, we managed to get out, me and my boys." She took her phone out and showed Liza a few photos. The little one had her eyes and nose. The firstborn bore little resemblance to Annie.

"Here I am. Back to nothing. At least, we made it out in time. One day more, and it would have been a casket flying back here," Annie said, trying to laugh it off. A glance at her cheap plastic watch signaled the end of their reunion. "Well, break's over. It was nice seeing you, Liza. What do you say we go back to Laurel together soon?"

"Sure," Liza replied, although she knew the years apart had reduced the invitation to a turn of phrase. Even so, they exchanged numbers and promised to keep in touch.

Walking home now, Liza wished she hadn't met Annie. She wished she hadn't heard the story that had her so deep in thought, she crossed a red light. Curse her gossip-hungry mind for forcing her to stay back at that 7-Eleven. Liza couldn't imagine the pan-wielding husband without seeing

Christopher's face.

Annie's stories lingered in her mind when Christopher called to ask about her day. Was she counting down the days until his visit? Was she as excited as he was? Was she having trouble sleeping through the excitement? Liza was in too foul a mood to carry a conversation outside of yes, no, grunt, sigh. Tonight, there was none of the lively chatter. No talk about woodwork. No high-pitched giggles. Awkward pauses crept and wove into short replies. They usually talked for hours, hanging up only because Christopher had to go to work or Liza had to get some sleep. Tonight, they kept it short and not so sweet.

"Babe, I need to go. I'm going out with my friends." Liza couldn't unsee Christopher stubbing out a cigarette on her wrist. Or hitting her with a frying pan. Or maiming her on the side of the head with a wood plank. She needed to be around friends. She needed a distraction from the raging storm inside her. Sure, they'd badger her about her unemployment. But if they managed to pull her out of this mood, then she'd gladly pay the price.

***

Jo watched the whole thing with curiosity. She had grown accustomed to Liza's chat sessions with Christopher. She'd learned to be familiar with it, as much as the fake floral scent of disinfectant spray and the regular changing of bed sheets in the apartment. Besides, her house was a tiny space. It was difficult to escape their exchanges of sweet nothings and sexual innuendos. If Jo wanted to block out updates on their boring couple things, she would have to live outside.

"That was fast," Jo remarked.

"Yeah. Too tired today."

"You want to bail on this Appliance Center thing? We could

stay in."

"But you're already dressed."

"I strip real quick."

Jo meant it as a joke, but Liza wasn't having it. At the end of it all, Liza insisted on going. They arrived at the Appliance Center a little after eleven, the entrance already locked up. Minutes after Liza dialed a number on her phone, the steel grills were raised enough to let them in. Jo appreciated the cleverness of it all. Movie night after shopping hours. Taking advantage of these high-end TVs and home theaters. A few throw pillows and blankets from the Home Section people upstairs. What's a couple hours of entertainment on the boss's tab? They even had a small cooler with beers and soda. Jo fended for herself, while Liza walked around and caught up with a few people. Jo chatted with Randy, a sales clerk who had worked with Liza in the past.

"Hard worker, that one. Tough luck we can't stay for very long in one place," he said, shaking his head. "But, hey, with that boyfriend of hers, Liza should be out of here soon. I can feel it."

Jo nodded along, hoping Randy wouldn't ask her about the latest Christopher scoop. Couldn't a girl have a break from the Christopher talk? Luckily, Randy didn't pursue the matter further.

"Aren't you scared of getting caught?" Jo asked to change the subject, nodding at the CCTV cameras repeated all over the ceiling.

"Not if you got the CCTV guy freezing the frames for you." Randy pointed to a man in a twisted-gray shirt, a black snapback crowning his head.

"That's your CCTV guy?"

"Yeah. Why?"

"Nothing. He doesn't look like a CCTV guy to me."

Jo's had her fill of nerdy, four-eyed IT guys. This one broke the mold. He wore a full, well-trimmed beard. Tattoos covered both his arms. Jo ogled the skinny jeans, tight enough to foreshadow what was lying underneath. *To be eaten*, Jo mentally filed away as she eyed the CCTV guy again from top to bottom. For now, her main mission was to pick Liza up from this uncharacteristically dark mood she was in. She excused herself from Randy, popped open two beers from the cooler and found Liza slumped against a wall, knees bent, legs a little bit apart. She was smoking a cigarette.

"Don't tell me the fire alarm's turned off, too," Jo said, pointing at a sprinkler.

"Wanna know a secret? They're never on."

The lights dimmed, and the party of about twenty huddled around the biggest TV Jo had ever seen. Not even the mistress's flat-screen was as big as this. Jo could stretch her arms on both sides and it still wouldn't be as long. It blared to life, the somber instrumental of a horror flick filling the air. Jo sat through the first thirty minutes of the movie and its predictable plot before her attention started to wander. Her eyes scanned the room for Mr. CCTV. He was standing beside a row of microwave ovens, leaning like the cool cat that he was. She meant to make a move when a woman showed up beside him, appearing from the row of oven toasters. She gave him a few pecks on the neck. CCTV Guy was apparently spoken for.

"Beat to it," Jo grumbled, chugging her beer, half-expecting Liza to chime in with a curious "Who is it now?" No response. Liza directed a blank stare towards the screen. Jo shifted to face Liza, snapping her fingers at her.

"Okay, quiet you is scaring the fuck out of me. Spit it out."

Liza forced a smile and returned her attention to the TV. It didn't take long for the movie to pick up on the gore. Bright red from the TV mixed with the bluish darkness of the Appliance Center. Liza's face turned into a ghastly shade of purple.

"Okay. Now, that is scary," Jo said, pointing at Liza's pained smile. That, at least, earned her a punch on the arm. Jo waited for Liza's false bravado to run its course. Soon enough, Liza's head fell like dead weight on Jo's shoulder. They didn't talk for a while. They were content to hold hands and watch the movie like everyone else. Jo was uncomfortable with the silence and the prolonged hugging, but she didn't feel like wriggling out of this. She had a sense Liza needed some comfort right about now.

"It's Christopher, isn't it?"

"Do you think Christopher's a monster?"

The slasher flick was at its home stretch. The last chase through the woods, complete with a grim musical score. The couples clutched each other, melding into one single blob. The single ones made do with a frightened group hug. CCTV guy wasn't paying attention to the movie; he was still getting pecked, to Jo's dismay.

"Where did that come from?"

Liza told her about Annie from Laurel. Funny they were having this conversation now. Jo had long feared that Christopher might be a monster. He may be cut from the same cloth as the other failed relationships Liza had weathered through the years. Every single time Liza mentioned Christopher, Jo braced for the worst. Another American bites the dust. The longer it lasted, the longer it would take for Liza to recover. It was better for her to cut her losses now and make a break for it. Now, this Annie was a cautionary tale that Jo could goad Liza on. It could turn Liza off this American dream for good, convince her that it's safer to stay here and try her luck.

For some reason, Jo chose not to. Besides, this Christopher person was flying to meet her. That was a first. That ought to count as good effort, right?

"Remember the waterfall in Laurel? You begged me not to jump because I could hit my head, fall into a coma, and die? Or crack my ribs, puncture a lung, and bleed to death?"

"And, you jumped anyway."

"I jumped anyway. It was better than sex, Liza. And that's saying a lot, coming from me. To think I almost let you talk me out of it!" Jo reminded herself that this was not her story. She shifted the conversation back to Liza. "Thing is, the past fourteen men you dated, it felt like you only needed them for the green card. A few hundred dollars in the wallet every now and then. Christopher, you don't simply need him. You love him. And, that's scary. You think about the fourteenth, may his soul rot in purgatory, and imagine Christopher doing that to you. That alone would kill you. How much more this husband from hell you told me about?"

The pro-Christopher sentiment surprised them both. What now? Was Jo suddenly the president of Christopher's Solid Gold fan club? No, not really. Jo was the president of Liza's Solid Gold fan club. She was a fan of every version of her. This sulky, making-do-with-a-lukewarm-beer, overthinking version was not an exception.

"True, he could be a monster, Liza. He could be up there on the evil scale, next to the money-hungry bastard who owns this place. As evil and uncivilized and woman-hating as the president. This online dating thing could be some sociopathic outlet to him. See how far he goes to pass as normal until he gets the chance to stab you fifty-five times in your sleep. But you forget that you're only half of the equation. You forget that this is new to him, too."

Liza rolled her eyes, confused at what Jo was driving at. "Christopher's forty-five. He's hardly a rookie."

"You don't get it, do you?" Sometimes, Liza thought too much for her own good. She made small things more complicated than they actually were.

"Get what?"

"It's new because it's you," Jo said, too softly, too slowly. She recovered the firmness in her voice, lest the soft and slow be mistaken for tenderness. She cleared her throat and continued, her tempo picking up, restoring the matter-of-fact quality to her voice.

"Because, the moment he sees you, you won't be some photo to him anymore. Not some far-off place anymore. Not a girl in a tiny square on his phone. He will live your world, Liza. See what you see. Walk where you walk. And if he's half the decent man you say he is, sociopath or no, he will not be able to help himself. He will be bound to do right by you. He will give you the softer side of the bed. Even if it means he has to sleep with rusty springs digging at his back or the sun burning a hole on his face every morning. He'll make you breakfast and get your coffee right—two tablespoons each of sugar and creamer—every single time. He will sing you to sleep when you wake up from a nightmare. If he's got pipes like mine, that is. I mean, not to brag, but you know how good I am at the singing shit."

Liza looked at Jo, her gaze both curious and perplexed. Jo could see the warmth returning to Liza's cheeks. The worries were dissipating. The night was turning itself around. She wondered if Liza knew that she spoke the truth. None of it was soapboxing or acting or turning on the charm. Every bit of it was true.

Jo kissed Liza on the other cheek, hoping it was enough to keep her fears at bay. The darkness seemed to act like an inertial force, pushing Liza towards her. Liza hovered close to Jo's face. Jo contemplated what this stirring inside her meant. Was she the only one who felt it? The darkness offered no answers but kept pushing Liza forward. She inched closer and closer until Jo couldn't help but part her lips for her.

But then, the darkness disappeared, its force on Liza dying along with it. The ceiling was suddenly bathed in white show-room light. The space filled with chatter. A gang of boys haggled with each other for the last few beers. A couple complained about the movie, lamenting if they could have a John Lloyd movie next time. Jo and Liza blinked, as if waking up from a trance of their own conjuring. They shielded their faces from the light and from each other. They were keen on restoring the space between them; it didn't matter how awkwardly they went about it. Jo crawled away on all fours before standing up to get another beer, a can of Coke, a bowl of chips, any excuse to walk to the far end of the room. Liza shifted towards a corner to light another cigarette.

Jo scooped some cold water from the cooler and doused her face with it.

Chapter 5

On the ride home, there was no mention of what happened or didn't happen at the Appliance Center. In the days that followed, Jo thought of broaching the subject whenever she caught Liza staring at her from across the room. But nothing came of it. Liza seemed intent on putting the matter to rest, and Jo was only too willing to follow suit. Liza made up with Christopher and got back to their marathon sessions. For a week before Christopher's visit, all they talked about was Christopher's itinerary. Jo heard mentions of Coron and Cebu. The day Christopher came, Liza asked Jo if she could accompany her to the airport.

"No, I don't want to go to the airport with you," Jo said with a groan. She could only imagine how insufferable a day with them would be, now that they were in the same time zone. She would rather do errands than get stuck with the lovebirds.

"But, come on, Jo. Please? I want you to meet Christopher."

"I really need to get my medical clearance, Liza."

"Three tapa dates and three shawarma dates. One all-you-can-eat dinner when I get a proper job."

Jo groaned again, finding it difficult to resist such a sweet deal. And Liza's puppy-dog eyes. "Fine. Wait for me after my errands. If I don't make it before five, just go without me."

For her errands, Jo shuttled to Meralco to pay for electricity. She walked to 7-Eleven for the water bill, then hailed a pedicab to the nearest mall to get her cranky pocket Wi-Fi fixed. It was past lunch by the time she reached the clinic for her medical clearance. Jo took great pains to not get pregnant and made sure that she was always healthy and up for the job.

There was no mistaking this clinic for St. Luke's. No guard in a crisp white polo barong to greet you a good day. No natural-light, open-space lobby to hang out in while you waited for lab results. There was air conditioning, a lone split-type, more often busted than not. A matronly, gray-haired receptionist manned the front desk. Everything in this clinic was old, wrinkled, and crumbling. Jo chipped old paint from a nearby wall. Up front, the clinic advertised itself as a maternity and lying-in center. In the back rooms, it performed abortions. Jo came here because fees were cheap. Because of the late hour, the line had already snaked around the cramped reception area. Jo took a seat beside a woman in her mid-thirties, who kept wringing her hands and pulling at the stray hair behind her ear.

"That's what you get for selling yourself. If you got yourself a proper job, you wouldn't have to get an abortion," the receptionist mumbled, flipping a chart of records. The woman gasped as if struck in the face, before looking down and hiding her face behind clasped hands. As if she wasn't perfectly clear the first time, the receptionist looked at the woman, turning up her nose in a show of disgust. "Whose is that? Some drug addict on the street corner, I bet."

"Oy, *manang*, can you stop it with the side comments and nasty side eye?" Jo said loudly. More than a few heads perked up to see what the fuss was about. "We're having a bad enough time waiting and making do with this shithole clinic. We don't need your shaming to make it worse than it is."

A hush descended on the waiting room. The receptionist glared at Jo before going back to her chart-flipping. The woman beside Jo gave her a slight smile. Jo responded with a wink and offered the woman her spare bottle of water.

"Thank you," the woman mouthed, taking a small gulp of water. "Here for an abortion, too?"

"Oh, no. Just the good old regular checkup."

"With groping."

"With groping," Jo agreed.

"Look at us, at the front line of all the diseases on these posters, and we can't even get checked for free. Not even a health card to cover, you know, the hazards. And, an abortion doesn't come cheap, I'll tell you that. The pains of this job, a free checkup sounds about right."

"Well, we're not exactly a legal profession," Jo said, her flippant demeanor giving way to a look of indignation. "But it's about time we are. About fucking time. Make this legal and regulated, know what I'm saying? And how about not throwing us in jail for working it. That's a start."

The receptionist called another name. The woman looked to be out of her teens, reminding Jo of her virgin poet ad. She was pregnant but the bump barely showed, thanks to the loose navy-blue shirt she was wearing. Jo watched one of the nurses guide her to the back room.

"Say, have you ever been pregnant?"

Jo shook her head. "No. I have an irrational fear of getting knocked up. My worst nightmare is having another me running about." She gave a short chuckle and shrugged. "I can't even handle my own self sometimes."

"Not even pregnancy scares?"

Jo dismissed the notion with a wave of the hand. "Less scares if you're always safe. I take pills. My condom rule is non-negotiable. Get that thing packed in latex or you don't get any. I do a background check, too. Just because you pay for my service does not mean you can be gross and careless with this." She flipped her hand up and down, gesturing at her body. "Only fair, way I see it. They're checking me up, too, anyway."

The woman sighed again. "I wish I had your self-control. Guy triples my rate for no condom and unli-pops, how could I refuse? I usually got away with it. Considered myself lucky." Her hand trailed down to rub the small bump below her stomach. "Not this time. And it sucks, but I can't keep it. I'm already stretching myself thin working for my kids."

Fidgeting in her seat to fish out a wallet from her back pocket, she took out a photo of a boy and a girl. The older one was dark-skinned and missing two front teeth, the younger with a full head of wavy hair and an innocent stare. "Seven and three. Parting gifts from my dead husband, bless his soul."

"Got a pimp?"

"Yes. He's not so bad. Fairer than most."

"No pimp is ever fair enough. Quit that pimp. That's what you can do."

As if reading Jo's mind, the woman shook her head and explained why she hadn't tried freelancing yet. "I'm scared of doing it alone. What if I can't close deals? What if I price too high or too low? I can't risk not taking home money—can't do that to my kids. At least, my pimp tells me where to go and I get paid, sure thing, no matter if it's small." She raised her hands in defeat. "And, those online-online things! I'm too old for it!"

"I could teach you," Jo said with a shrug.

A rare uptick of a grin crossed the woman's face. "Not worried

I'd steal your clients?"

"There's a lot to go around online, believe me. A whole lot in need of a good fuck or sometimes just someone to talk to. Besides, I didn't say I'd teach you everything." Sensing the woman's interest in the subject, Jo started talking about how she got into sex work. They were starting to warm up to each other when the receptionist called Jo's name.

"Suarez, Joanna?"

"Well, I guess that's me." They exchanged names and numbers, inking the contract of a new friendship. The woman shook Jo's hand. "Call me if you change your mind about that fair pimp of yours," Jo said, enclosing *fair* in air quotes.

"Good luck with the perv," the woman said, referring to the eighty-year-old dinosaur OB-GYN.

"Tell me about it," Jo said, rolling her eyes. She patted the woman on the thigh, wished her luck, and stood up. She gave the receptionist the finger, sticking her tongue out, before walking to the narrow, poorly lit hallway towards the examination room.

After a handsy body exam from Dr. Pervysaurus Rex, Jo finally earned her clean bill of health. Despite the long day, she derived a sense of fulfillment from being able to pay her bills and set her life in order. Days like this reminded her how far she had come. She was no longer at the mercy of Mama-san or some cheapskate pimp. She read stories about women like her that would break even the coldest of hearts. Drowned in the toilet. Shipped off on a fishing boat to God knows where. Deported with scars on their bodies, or worse. She was lucky she'd got out, escaping that raid the way she did. Sure, this freedom came with an endless slew of bills. But it meant that there was something to work for. Bills meant she had a house to keep, even if it was tiny and bare. She wasn't sleeping over with friends anymore or spending nights passed out in exhaustion for meager tips at the bar.

She got home and found Liza scurrying about, in a hurry. Her wet hair was in a ponytail. Jeans were unbuttoned. Her off-white button-down could have used a few passes under the hot iron.

"Oh, thank god you're here. Have you seen my red heels?"

"Under the bed?"

Liza crouched to find the red heels, sitting there all this time. Once she had the red heels, she asked for the black clutch next. She wanted the matte red lipstick. She removed her blouse and ironed it until it was as boxy and straight as her work uniform. All it needed was a sprinkle of starch to stand strong in a signal number 4 storm.

"You've ironed the life out of that shirt."

"What? Is it ugly? Is it the wrong shirt? Should I wear this instead?" Liza asked, picking up a white cut-off with a "Go Fuck Your Selfie" print in front.

"First off, that's mine. You sure your inner neat freak can handle a ratty cut-off with stray threads at the hem? Second, it's going to be fine."

"I'm so nervous."

Jo grabbed Liza by the arms and steadied her. "This is fine. This is you—neat, in control, badass, confident." She flipped open a few of the buttons on Liza's blouse, spread the collar a little bit wider. "But angling to get laid."

Liza laughed, sending a brief flutter to the pit of Jo's stomach. What was that about? This was a moment when they should have hugged it out. But owing to the night at the Appliance Center, they stood where they were. Not an inch closer.

"You ready?" Liza asked.

Jo nodded. "Question is, are you?"

Chapter 6

She was ready for this, or so she told herself. Liza pushed her way into the expectant throng of people near the arrival gate. She fought for a spot by the metal railings, displacing a big-boned, curly-haired woman. The woman looked her up and down before leaving. How many of these people were like her, nervous about meeting their boyfriends for the first time? Liza wished she had brought a placard like the others. She cursed herself for not planning this well enough, and wiped her forehead with cold, clammy hands. Jo gently clutched her shoulder, encouraging her to calm down. The digital clock at the arrival gate displayed half past eight. Christopher should be here any minute.

"Why isn't he here yet?"

"Relax. eight p.m. means nine p.m. at the airport. You know that."

"You think he'll show up at all?"

"You looking like that?" Jo said, giving Liza a once-over. "I mean, shit, I would."

Thank God for Jo's dry humor and emergency pick-me-ups. Liza smiled and gave Jo's hand a tight squeeze.

After much fidgeting and waiting and elbowing, Liza saw Christopher at last. His six-foot frame towered over the porters and guards. His hair was slicked back and gleaming with gel. His sky-blue T-shirt hugged him at the shoulders and arms. She watched him push a luggage trolley, looking around for a familiar face.

"Christopher!" she cried, flailing her two hands like a distress signal for help. "Christopher, over here!"

Liza held her breath as their eyes met. Did she disappoint him with the way she looked? She had sent him tons of pictures. But what if she wasn't what he expected? Did he imagine her to be taller, or with fuller breasts, or longer legs? Was she too loud in calling his name? Was she too eager? Was her lipstick too much, too red? Liza's heart could burst with all this anxiety. But then, dispelling her worries, Christopher's mouth broke into a grin. When he waved his hand, Liza waved back. The trolley clacked against the concrete as Christopher made his way to her.

"Oh, wow. That is way too much gel," Jo muttered, earning a sharp elbow to the ribs from Liza.

"Hi," Christopher said, kissing Liza on the cheek and holding her in his arms. For the first time that day, Liza felt calm. Her heartbeat slowed back to normal. Christopher had made it to her. There was no need to worry now.

Christopher had booked a hotel in Manila, a short ride from Jo's apartment. It was a boutique hotel tucked between the high-end skyscrapers along Roxas Boulevard. While Jo was pretty much the GPS of hotels, motels, and transient inns in the metro, Liza was the opposite. She rarely entered these hotels with their high chandeliers and grand pianos. The marbled tiles were so shiny, they threw her ogling face back at her.

"The Casa del Sol. Plus points for good taste," Jo whispered to Liza, while Christopher settled his reservation with the receptionist.

"So, you like him now?"

"Scale slid a bit, yeah." Jo said with a wink.

Dinner was less of an awkward affair with Jo there. Liza started to relax, what with the good food, the warm chandeliers above them, and the soft music from the grand piano. She could hear Jo humming along between mouthfuls of rice and steak.

"So, where you lovebugs off to on this romance trip?"

"Coron. Cebu. A weekend in Laurel," Christopher responded.

"Laurel! Don't miss out on the waterfalls."

Liza wagged a hand and reached for Jo across the table, remembering one of their trips to her hometown. Jo had walked up a thirty-foot waterfall, despite Liza's fair share of warnings and threats and protests. "When you jumped, you almost gave me a heart attack. And then, you took your sweet time going up. I thought you'd drowned or broke a rib and died!"

"Don't miss it, Christopher. It's..." Jo closed her eyes and clutched her chest. She shook her head slowly, as if savoring the memory. "Oh, better than sex, it is. And to think that one almost talked me out of it."

"I was only looking out for you. What if you fell all wrong and broke your skull on a sharp rock?"

"Morbid 24/7, Christopher. I tell you. Get used to it."

Liza stuck out her tongue at Jo. Christopher cleared his throat and took a swig of beer. Silence crept between snippets of small, inconsequential conversation about life in the U.S., comparing public transport and roads and buildings, and their own families. It got interesting when Jo started throwing slam-book questions at the table. They had a hoot confessing about first crushes and first kisses. They winced at each other's weirdest sex stories.

"Oh, Jo, Jo, Jo! Tell her about the dentist!" Liza urged, before turning to Christopher. "Babe, you have to hear this one."

"That's too weird for a first meeting, Liza." Jo said, shaking her head, but already laughing.

"Oh, come on, don't stop now," Christopher said, trying to get on this current train of conversation.

"That's what she said!" Jo and Liza shrieked at the same time.

Jo conceded, leaning forward and giving the table a good tap. "OK. So, there's this dentist. Clean as all fuck. Attractive, too. I'd fuck him for free, that kind of hot. Only he had a very job-specific fetish. He would only get a rise if toothpaste foam was dripping out of my mouth. So, yeah. I'd have to brush my teeth first. Then, minty foam in my mouth, I'd have to go down on him. And, right after he comes, he would always say..."

"Now, gargle!" Liza finished, laughing and slapping the table with her fists. They were getting strange looks from the other patrons. Christopher fidgeted in his seat and kept looking at his watch. He called the waiter to bill them out.

Jo picked up on the hint and made up an alibi. She stretched her arms, faking a yawn. She clapped her hands and announced her graceful exit from the meet-and-greet. "It's getting late. And I have an ad tomorrow morning. So, I'm gonna leave you two lovebirds to your icky lovebirdy things. Do your thing and be safe, okay?"

"I'll walk you out," Liza offered. She turned to give Christopher a kiss. "Room 908, right? I'll meet you there."

Down the street, a few late-night pedicabs still roamed about. To her right, pink lights blinked "GIRL BAR" and "HAPPY HOUR" alternately. A jeepney sputtered by, leaving a cloud of dark smoke in its wake.

"Thank you, Jo. I know you didn't want to go, but you did. Thank you."

"Spare me the drama. I was in it for the free steak." Jo rubbed her tummy and gave it a couple of pats.

"Liar."

Jo's face softened, a rare smile lighting up her face. "Yeah, I was in it for you."

All awkwardness forgotten, Liza held her and almost didn't want to let go. She nursed this funny feeling in her chest, of wanting to go home with Jo. Have a smoke by the window and talk about the silliest things. She thought of Christopher waiting in his room. She thought of the night ahead. Anxiety started to make her head throb again.

"You'll be fine. He looks like a great guy."

Liza stood by the sidewalk and waved goodbye as Jo chased a nearby jeepney. Jo stuck her head out of the window to flash a thumbs-up. Crazy little monkey, what would Liza do without her? Liza smoked a cigarette and looked up at the pattern above her. Yellow rooms. Pitch-black spaces. Half-drawn curtains. Fully opened drapes. Silhouettes looking out. Shadows dancing inside. Room 908, was it now? She counted the panes and tried to guess where the ninth floor was.

First-time jitters. That was all there was to this giddy feeling swirling inside her.

Right?

Right, Liza told herself before slowly walking back to the lobby.

Chapter 7

The days could not be any slower for Jo. With Liza leaving for her so-called romance tour—Liza's words, not hers—the house slunk back to its emptiness. She had been living alone for years, gone through Liza staying for only weeks at a time. This shouldn't be an issue, no big deal. Business as usual. But the gloom that followed Jo around begged to differ.

"Where are you now?"

"Coron. Just got home from beach hopping. It's so beautiful here! The beach, the hot springs, the lakes, everything—I wish I didn't have to go back to Manila."

The little monkey finally called, three days into her Coron leg of the Liztopher Romance Tour. Again, Liza's words, not hers, never hers. Love team branding was Liza's kink. For fifteen minutes and counting, Liza had been regaling Jo with stories of the week that was. Liza complained about the rough plane ride that allegedly added ten years to her age. Jo drowned out the details to a make-out session with Christopher in a secret cove. When Liza described the cool blues and greens of the water, Jo could taste the salt in her mouth and the fresh ocean spray on her skin. The excitement in Liza's voice was infectious, soothing the bone-tired ache from Jo's string of bookings. She had gotten used to coming home to that voice, to the life and color that Liza brought. Jo missed her now that she wasn't around.

"Then, we went to this secret bar. Tiny and dark as all hell. Owned by a man, thin, wiry, with dreads down to his waist. There was only a narrow wooden ladder to get to it. Inside, it looked like the one you used to work in! I was so worried they'd raid the place!"

At the mention of her old workplace, reds and pinks began to fill Jo's mind. She pictured a couple making out in a dark corner. Or a loner nursing a sweating glass of rum. Liza raved about a trio of Spanish tourists who took over the instruments in the bar. There were guitars, drums, an African horn that took some mad skill to make good music with. Jo remembered the upbeat dance-craze songs she used to perform lap dances to.

"He asked me to dance."

Jo snorted at the image of Liza dancing. Liza was a no-quit go-getter, but dancing had always stayed a little bit out of her reach. She'd once sprained her ankle trying to learn Jo's striptease routine. They weren't even near close to the good part.

"Oh no. Tell me you got out of that one."

"You're thinking of the time I sprained my ankle, aren't you?"

"You know me too well."

"Joke's on you because Christopher thought I was an amazing dancer," Liza said with a haughty scoff at the end.

Jo raised her eyebrows in amused disbelief. "Oh, did he now?"

"The way he looked at me, Jo," Liza said, her tone shifting to soft and dreamy. "It was as if I was the only person in the room. The other women were staring at him like they had plans to steal him from under me. But he made sure I felt wanted, that he wanted nobody else."

"Here comes the cheesefest. Let me warm up some pan de

sal."

Liza laughed, that raspy sound, almost always out of breath, like every chuckle would be her last. "You and your heart of stone. I had a feeling you'd say that. But, oh Jo, I wish you were here, though."

"Like hell you need me. Where are you off to next again?" Jo deflected, pursing her lips to stop from smiling. Her heart lurched repeatedly, beating fast and hard against her skin.

"Cebu. Christopher says he wants to check out the architecture there. Old churches and old houses and historical stuff. He has a checklist. Can you believe it?"

"And, what are you going to check out?"

"I kinda like churches. Reminds me of home. So, I'm looking forward to that. What else? Cebu lechon and street food, of course. Christopher, of course. Every single inch of him, if you know what I mean."

"Atta girl," Jo said, her attempt at pep talk hardly inspiring. "Tired?"

"Yeah," Jo said. There was no other explanation to the flat reply. It must be fatigue. Gotta be. "A good night's sleep should do it."

"Don't tire yourself out, please. Eat. Sleep. See you soon, Joanna! I miss you."

In the next call, Jo tried a better hand at enthusiasm. She endured the opening salvo, another three-minute monologue-slash-complaint. This time, it was about how sore Liza's feet were. Liza had visited so many churches that she could go on a *visita iglesia* twice over. Christopher was an absolute geek about the old architecture. Liza shared photos of him at Magellan's Cross, neck craned, camera at the ready. He said it was for inspiration, designs to try back home.

"Christopher walked out to get a drink. I stayed back. Too tired," Liza said, massaging her sore feet. "It feels like Manila here. Any ads today?"

"No. I saw the mistress today for lunch," Jo said before quickly adding, "Other than the swollen heels, what went down with you two?"

Liza bit her lip and clapped her hands a couple of times. Something was weighing on her mind.

"Better out than in, they say."

"There was a weird thing at lunch. We were eating our lechon in peace, right? Out of the blue, he asked me how many kids I wanted if we get married."

"And, you said, 'put a ring on this first, sucker,' right? I mean, there's no other response to that." Jo wagged her hand a la Beyoncé, her mouth forming an exaggerated pout. Her shoulders shimmied to the hum of "Single Ladies."

"Wait, do you think he's going to propose?"

"What did he say?"

"When I asked him why, he shrugged and then kept himself busy with the food. He didn't bring it up the rest of the afternoon. Then, soon as we came back to the hotel, he said he wanted to get a drink. He looked relieved that I was staying behind. Weird, right?"

Jo rubbed her chin, eyebrows furrowed, pretending to give the matter a serious ponder. "Maybe he's testing you. Maybe he wants three kids, no more, no less, and wanted to know if you want three kids, too. If not, he'd just ghost you and find himself a Cebuana he can have three kids with."

"You know, I sometimes ask myself why you're my best friend. The cigarette peddler downstairs said we look good together, Christopher and me. Maybe I should make him my best friend, instead."

"I'm your best friend because I'm funny."

"Not by a long shot."

"I keep it real."

"That, I'd give you that."

"Admit it, Liza. You love me."

"I do love you, you weirdo."

There was that lurch again. Jo couldn't blame it on fatigue this time; it was a day off, and she had been in bed all day. She sat up from the bed, her body tense, like someone just rammed a steel rod right up her spine. Static silence made her head swell tenfold, as Liza waited for her to continue the banter. She had no snappy retort in hand, which frazzled her nerves even more. Desperate for a sound, any sound to pass between them, Jo cleared her throat.

"How many did you say you wanted?"

"Four. Three always leaves someone rotten."

"Oh, shit, Liza. He'd definitely ghost you now."

"Will you marry me if he does?"

"Over your ghosted body."

Chapter 8

Since that conversation when she was in Cebu, there hadn't been a single text or call from Liza. Had something happened? Had Jo's half-joke become true? Had Christopher ghosted her? Snapping on her bra and appraising her face in the mirror, Jo pushed Liza out of her mind and returned to work. She had just finished stripper duties at a stag party. The party had long gone home, and she was the only one left to spend the night with the bachelor.

It wasn't that big a party, only ten or fifteen, but these rich boys sure knew how to have a good time. Beer bottles were strewn everywhere, along with bottles with labels that Jo only knew a few of. There was Cuervo; she hated that shit. Jack Daniel's, yes. Absolut, only if it came without the flavors. Crepe paper confetti and glitter from a party-popper cake stuck to every surface. Jo almost had to rub her skin raw to get them off. Ashtrays were overflowing, and not only with the filter end of cigarettes. By the coffee table sat a box of condoms. *Class Act. For the gentleman in you!*

The ad was half-decent now, a fresh white polo on top and gray boxers below the waist. They had been at it for a couple of hours when he asked for a break. He sat on the couch and reached for the bottle of Absolut. He poured a little bit into two clean red cups, ones he deemed clean anyway, and called Jo to sit beside him. They raised their glasses for a toast.

"Fuck me, that hit the spot," Jo said with a wince and a throaty groan.

"Say that again."

Jo stretched her legs from the opposite end of the couch. "So, what's your real story?"

The ad ruffled his wavy brown hair, chuckling to himself. He smoothed his shirt and started playing with the cuffs. "What makes you think I have a story? I could be another boring rich man. You've had men like me before, I take it. Granted, I stand to inherit an agri-business after this wedding. Still, could be boring."

"Let me be the judge of boring. Everyone's got a story." Jo tapped him on the knee. "Give me that soap opera–type shit. I haven't had good TV in forever."

"You have got to be the weirdest stag party stripper I have ever met. Where did Adrian get you again?" he said, his gray eyes holding a tinge of humor, looking straight at Jo. "You really want my story?"

"Give it to me."

He nodded slowly, running a smooth hand up and down Jo's leg, seeming to digest the question into an answer. "My story is I don't want to be like my dad. Or my uncle. Or my grandpa." He laughed at the confusion on Jo's face. "We're a family of second families. All the men are cheating, have cheated, will be cheating. Some of my uncles married for the connections, for the business. Then they took their pleasure somewhere else far away from home. I've been quite the playboy. She made me not want to be. Break the cycle, know what I mean?"

Jo poured another shot of Absolut into her red cup. "So, she changed you," she said, with a snap of her fingers. "Just like that."

"I guess? I'm done fucking around. I mean, have you seen her?" The ad was going to marry this socialite-slash-model-slash-painter-slash-actress. Not Jo's type, but they would make a lot of pretty babies. "I love her. I want to take care of her, do all things right for her, be that person she goes to in her mind. God knows she's all I think about."

That go-to person in the mind thing again. "Hold up. I'm getting a flashback from another ad. Shit, man. You're the second person—let's not count my best friend—who's told me that. I'm starting to think this is a pathetic fad I'm somehow missing out on."

The ad sat up from the end of his couch, crossing his legs. This turn in the conversation had piqued his interest. "You don't think of anyone? Not even a celebrity? Not even when you're all alone? Come on. I find that hard to believe."

What is it with these people? There was no need to go all sappy about sex. Sex was about the body responding to instinct. It was reflex. Touch where it burns, provoke and prolong what feels good, stop when it hurts. There was no need to overthink the situation, to go sentimental about it. Sex was a binary switch most of the time, anyway. You feel it or you don't. You want it or you don't.

"But it's so much better that way!" the ad argued before throwing Jo a playful wink. "Do you want to try?"

"I thought you were all tapped out."

"Try it. If it doesn't work, I'll pay you double."

"Better cough it up now."

Jo rolled her eyes, threw him a packet of Class Act and followed him back to the bedroom. They undressed like there was an all-must-go memo on clothes, but took it slow once they hit the bed. He was gentler this round, taking his time and waiting for Jo to build. Jo felt so bad at how hard he was trying to prove this theory that she wanted to fake an orgasm to please him. God knew it wouldn't be the first time. He closed his eyes, and Jo caught him smiling when he kissed her hand. He was probably already tuned to the fiancée on that mental TV of his. Jo was getting close now—props to him for holding out this far for her sake. It was Jo's turn to close her eyes. If this theory had any weight to it at all, she expected the mistress to appear in that navy-blue string bikini. After all, the mistress was the constant in a calendar crossed and filled out with strangers. It made the most sense, and was the only logical conclusion. The blank space behind her eyes began to fill, like a wonky TV slapped a few times into focus. It held Jo in suspense, like a curtain rising to reveal the magic trick.

Only, it wasn't the mistress she saw. It was Liza. Liza getting rid of that tight ponytail. Those standard-issue stockings. That boxy blue-and-white uniform. It was Liza in black underwear, feeling up Jo's thighs, nibbling on her ear, and whispering a soft but persuasive "Come on." Everything was Liza, and there was no escape. Jo tried to regain control. There had to be a switch somewhere to turn this off. A safe word to detach from this correlation. Disconnect these images from the orgasm building up and threatening to explode. She tried shaking her head, as if that were the secret password, as if Liza would ooze out of her ears and leave her be. She opened her mouth to say no, stop, no. But the words that came tumbling out were the exact opposite. She bucked up and screamed, and she felt her brain giving up, giving in. It was too late. She was too far gone.

"Well? What did you see?"

"Nothing. You wasted my shower for nothing, man." She rolled over and sat on the edge of the bed. She ruffled the curls of her hair and looked at him from her shoulder. "This hair? Takes a shit ton to dry. Now, I gotta go shower and do it again."

"Serious?"

"Would I lie to you?" But she was indeed lying, more to herself than her ad. He was wholly convinced that he was right. Jo wanted to humor him, pat him on the head like a good dog. But the results of his experiment were too upsetting to make fun of. Jo wasn't at all sure she wanted to grasp what it all meant. Why Liza, of all people? Liza over the mistress? Really?

"Strange. Well, as promised." He reached for his wallet and palmed Jo a sizable wad of thousand-peso bills. He then flopped on his belly—not his sexiest move of the night—and prepared to doze off. After getting back from the shower, Jo crept into bed and pulled the sheets over herself, up to her neck. She had been naked a thousand times before, but it had been a while since she felt the need to cover up. While her ad slept in peace, snoring lightly, Jo struggled between taking a nap and making sense of things. Her body demanded rest. But every time she closed her eyes, Liza filled up the blank space. For lack of a better solution, Jo sat at the balcony with a bottle of vodka for company. She left as soon as the first light of morning broke through the blinds.

Chapter 9

A voice was calling Jo's name, the scent of minty shampoo evoking a sense of familiarity in her. *Joanna*, the voice repeated. It was a singsong whisper that made her skin prickle; she could feel it on her stomach, on her face. After that wild stripper booking, all she wanted to do right now was sleep. She grunted, turned her back, and mumbled a few curses under her breath.

"Joanna!"

That got Jo waking up with a start, panic hitting her like an electric charge at seeing Liza hovering so close. She sprang back and rolled over in a hurry, falling off the bed and pulling the sheets with her. "I swear I wasn't dreaming of you! I swear!" Jo blurted out, much to Liza's confusion. "Wait, why are you here?"

"I just dropped Christopher off at the airport." Liza held out a hand and helped her up. She folded up the sheets while Jo tried to sort herself out, her brain most especially. "Hurry, get dressed. Let's eat at Mang Larry's, my treat!"

As always, Mang Larry's was already full of early lunch-goers. Taxi drivers. Construction workers. The hardcore foodies with their snatcher-worthy digital cameras. They scored a corner table near the sidewalk. Jo felt Liza's eyes on her, studying, trying to figure out what had happened while she was gone.

"What happened to you? You look like shit. Have you been sleeping like I told you to?"

"Don't start. I'm hungry," Jo said before any other words could be said, before Liza could ask if something had happened. She prayed Liza would leave it be, because *"Oh you know. No big deal. I just had the biggest orgasm in the history of my sorry-ass life and all thanks to a wet dream montage of you!"* wasn't exactly the go-to icebreaker during a casual lunch between friends.

Friends.

No more, no less.

A waitress came over to drop off an overflowing bowl of fried rice and tapa on their table. Jo sensed a celebration. They always marked life events here at this roadside *carinderia*. Breakups, Mang Larry's. First 10k client, Mang Larry's. First night with the mistress, Mang Larry's. Jo was hungry, but she couldn't eat a thing now. Every spoonful was like sandpaper to her throat, no matter how much water she downed it with. She couldn't look at Liza without feeling like she'd committed murder. Jo struggled to fight the giddiness radiating from her skull down to her stomach. The giddiness didn't come alone, though. It brought shame to the party, which left her feeling worse. When Liza squeezed her arm, the way she'd done a million times, it was like a thousand matchsticks set aflame on Jo's skin. She resisted the urge to scratch, to rub the feeling off her. But she didn't want to invite questions from Liza. So she made a frantic search for something else to focus on.

Jo found a cat trying to cross the street while Liza droned on about the progress of her job hunt. The cat moved two steps forward, then changed its mind as a motorcycle sped by. She glanced at Liza and noticed the gleam of happiness in her eyes, and all over her sunburned face. Jo focused back on the cat. It was halfway towards her now. Two more lanes to go until it could cross to the safety of the gutter. Jo rubbed her fingers in a come-hither gesture.

"Christopher proposed to me," Jo heard Liza say.

The cat froze, its tail all erect, back fur up and standing at attention. Jo clutched the edge of the table. She tried to breathe out the fear that forced her heart to clench. The source of her fear wasn't clear. Was it the cat? Was it Liza? Was it this suspended ache in her chest, hanging on to what Liza would say next? Liza paused to drink some water. She placed her left hand over Jo's. A tiny diamond ring gleamed tiny rainbows. It was out of place among the water-stained walls and the chink of cheap aluminum spoons. It didn't deserve Jo's unkempt hair and eleven-a.m. breath. It was so pretty, so painfully pretty, that Jo had to look away.

"I said yes."

The car swerved, evading the cat completely. The cat made it to their side of the road without becoming blood and guts and dirt-streaked fur on the asphalt. Instead, it was Jo who felt like roadkill, like the car had run right through her. She imagined her bones cracking upon impact. She pictured herself letting out a terrified yelp, stopped dead not by the force of 100 kph, but by the weight of three one-syllable words. *I said yes.* When something wet hit her cheeks, she thought for some reason that it was blood. When she wiped her face, there was no smear of red.

"Well, say something." Liza leaned closer, her left hand still holding Jo's. "Are those tears? Joanna, are you wasting tears for me?"

Jo quickly brushed the tears from her eyes. This was Liza's

moment; whatever mood cycle she was on right now did not matter. *Act normal, bitch.* She dialed back to a time before this engagement news, before that stupid sex dare with her ad, before these weird tear-inducing episodes. She turned her eyes to the road, watching the cars pass them by, before shifting her gaze back to Liza.

"Yeah, I'm so happy for you, Liza! Dream come true! Fucking finally, fifteenth time's the charm, eh?" Jo said, the cheer in her voice contrasting how flat and pathetic she felt inside. "What, you're gonna leave me now for the US of A?"

She faked a frown. It didn't feel fake at all.

***

In contrast to Liza's easy-breezy post-engagement bliss, Jo was having a hard time taking all this in. The days dragged on like months. She had a slow week—no ads at all —and being cooped up in the house wasn't helping improve her mood one bit. When the weekend rolled around bringing a mistress date with it, Jo was more than ready to get out of the house, away from Liza for a little while. She met the mistress at their favorite hotel in Ortigas. Same room, same time, like always. 321, corner suite, eight p.m. The mistress's husband was away again. It was always an out-of-the-country business trip or a golf charity event with him. Because they were on borrowed time, they never bothered with pleasantries. Their relationship was past small talk on how their days went and if they had missed each other. They did enjoy a good striptease now and then, especially the mistress. Tonight, though, Jo was operating on hyperspeed. No dirty murmurs either. In no time, a mismatch of clothes trailed them as they moved to the bedroom. The mistress's red-soled heels mixed with Jo's canvas sneakers. Her crop top mingled with a silk pencil skirt. Ripped pants piled over a soft, sheer button-down. Jo pushed her to the bed and lay on top of her, drawing circles on her skin with her tongue.

Everything was going well until Jo closed her eyes. It was a mistake, a trap she fell into, as Liza flooded her brain once more. She fought through it, labored to push Liza as far back in her mind as she could. But Liza kept coming back like a stubborn itch. Liza stayed there, in various levels of vividness, in different stages of undress. Jo tried so hard to shut her out that she barely felt the mistress's arm nudging her on the shoulder, shoving her away.

"Stop!" the mistress told Jo. Did she hear that right? Stop? Fuck, there was indeed a first time for everything. Jo blinked and backed away.

"You're not a good fuck when you're distracted."

Jo let out a frustrated sigh that had been a week in the making. She hid underneath the covers, embarrassed at not performing to her potential. This was her element. This and singing. Most people had a knack for art. Some people were walking encyclopedias. Liza was good at managing finances. Sex was one of the things Jo was reliable at. Now, with these flashes of Liza on her mind, she couldn't even do that.

"That obvious?"

"I brought some wine. It's in the fridge. Let me pour you some, and tell me what's making you such a sour fuck tonight," the mistress ordered. "For heaven's sake, dear, I can't have you like this."

Jo obeyed and walked to the kitchen. She pulled out the wine from the fridge and reached for a pair of glasses from the overhead cupboard. The mistress moved to the sofa, covered in a robe. Jo picked up her shirt and underwear from the pile on the floor. She sat cross-legged on the sofa as she watched

73

the mistress swirl the wine in the glass. Jo didn't bother about smelling the fruit and wood notes, and immediately helped herself to a healthy gulp.

"My best friend got engaged."

"Well, congratulations!" the mistress exclaimed. She raised her glass for a toast that Jo didn't bother to meet. "Unless we're not happy about that?"

"I don't know. I should be, right? Happy, I mean. Maybe not over the moon about it, but at least happy. Worst case, a positive reaction of some kind?"

"If not happy, then how do you feel about it?"

"Hot and bothered, more like."

"What could possibly bring that on, dear?"

"I may have had a few wet dreams about her," Jo confessed.

"That explains the hot," the mistress said. "Now, give me the bothered."

Jo had an image to maintain, an aura of invulnerability. Nothing ever fazed her. But she needed to talk to someone about this strange phenomenon, all these erratic reactions to everything Liza said and did lately. Getting some much-needed answers was greater than keeping up her cool and collected vibe.

"OK. Fine." Jo sighed and continued, "There's this dare an ad gave me. About having a person in your mind during sex. Supposed to make it so much better. And, I took him up on it. I know I shouldn't have. But I'm a sucker for a good wager. He was going to pay double, on top of the generous fee his friend paid me, right? So, I did it. And, I was so sure it was you I'd see if I ever saw anything."

"But it was this, this," the mistress said, urging Jo to supply the details.

"Liza," Jo answered.

The wine kept flowing, the bottle passing back and forth between the two of them.

"And then there was that almost-kiss at a party."

"You've probably had that moment with a hundred others."

"But this one's different." Jo paused, licking the bittersweet taste off her lips, trying to weave an explanation for why this was different from all the other almost-kisses she'd had. She came up with nothing.

"It's Liza," was all Jo could say. "I've always hoped she'd get engaged. I've seen her go through every failed relationship, and, you know what, it's exhausting. And then she finally tells me, right? Complete with the whole shoving the ring into my face kind of deal. And, I expected to be happy. Relieved." Jo waved her hands, as if she were a cheerleader holding crepe-paper pompoms. "Yay! A happy ending, about damn time!"

"But?"

"But it felt like a car crash through here." Jo poked at her sternum. "Crushing my insides until I couldn't breathe. Sat there while she told me all this, tears in my eyes. Tears!"

The mistress reached for her diamond earrings, looking away from Jo. She trained her gaze on a painting of a meadow. A man and a woman rested among purple wildflowers, faces turned towards a blue sky and the flight of birds in the distance. "Could you perhaps be in love with this Liza?"

"No. Fuck no. No fucking way," Jo said, shaking her head. She scoffed the idea out of the mistress's head, out of her own unreliable brain. Love, this kind of love the mistress was talking about, wasn't a thing to Jo. Happiness was something she could get on her own; she did not need anybody else for that. She was all she needed to be happy. The bad childhood and the fleeting romantic encounters also didn't help combat that belief. She scoffed again at the idea of being in love. What a horror show! But the more she tried to dismiss the idea, the less convincing her efforts became. The intended effects soon grew less violent. She could feel the mistress staring at her, observing every shift of emotion on her face. Jo felt a nagging pinprick in her chest. She tried drowning it with wine, finishing off a fresh glass in three gulps. But the pain refused to stay down. It coursed through her, throbbing, growing stronger the more she fought it.

"Could I be—"

The mistress shrugged and poured herself another glass. There was a touch of amusement in her eyes, like she was enjoying Jo's dilemma. Jo had never been this vulnerable around her before. The creased forehead. The childish pout. Two front teeth worrying obsessively at the lower lip. All brought on by the prospect of being in love.

A rather entertaining sight for the mistress. Not so much for Jo. She hated being at the mercy of her emotions. She directed them in others, not the other way around. With another gulp of wine, she decided that, whether this was indeed love or something else entirely, it had to go.

Chapter 10

*O*h, sorry, I'm booked until tomorrow evening.
Yeah, tonight won't do. I have a date.
Nope. You guessed it. Busy bee, you know me.

Prying Jo away from her new routine was a victory. Between ads, the mistress, and her current online dating romp, Jo was always out of the house. It looked to Liza like Jo was avoiding her. But whatever reason could make her want to do that? Liza caught Jo on a slow day and, with a little bit of arm-twisting, convinced her to people-watch by the harbor. Their favorite hobby. There was also a small café there Liza had been meaning to try.

Dusk was falling on the Manila Bay harbor. Couples were walking their dogs. Children were being corralled to a nearby pizza joint. The occasional senior citizen was doing some brisk walking by the breakwater. Jo paid little attention to any of this. She hunched over the pale glow of her phone, swiping her thumb left and right.

"How about this one?" Jo said, showing Liza the photo of a man with a braided beard and a full-sleeve tattoo. Lloyd, 32, Fairview, it said in the profile.

"Looks like he hasn't showered in days," Liza replied, offering a quick glance before taking a sip of her coffee. It was cheap and tasted exactly what she paid for. Like a boiled sock. She added milk. Dairy made anything less horrible.

Jo took her phone back. She resumed swiping and, after ten minutes, showed Liza another candidate. No beard. No tattoos. Hair brushed back and stayed by wax. "OK. This?"

"Too clean."

"The first one's too dirty. This one's too clean. There's no pleasing you today, huh?"

Liza clicked her tongue. She downed her coffee, dousing the mounting frustration before it could spread. It was their day; she'd worked hard to get this day, to squeeze it into Jo's hectic schedule. She didn't want to share this hard-earned day with mugshot strangers within a three-kilometer radius. Liza huffed loudly as Jo put down her phone and leaned back on the couch.

"Well, how about that one?" Jo said, looking at Liza's direction. Liza looked over her shoulder, still huffing, trying to find who it was now that caught Jo's attention. Great. Jo moved from strangers on a screen to real-life passersby. Liza went along with it and looked up and down the boardwalk.

"Where?"

"There. Faded highlights. A bit round at the waist. But, great boobs, can I just say?"

Liza was still looking out into the throng of people.

"Where? I can't find her."

"Right there! Dark brown eyes that could have you in a trance. Blushed cheeks even without makeup. Eyelashes so thick they look like falsies. A coffee stain by the corner of her mouth."

This got Liza wiping her mouth with a piece of tissue, finally getting the joke.

"Fuck you."

She had to clench her jaw to stop from smiling. Jo was still looking at her, a softness in her eyes. If this were a stranger, Liza would place that softness as longing. But this was Jo, after all. Jo didn't do feelings. Or did she now? Liza leaned forward, hand hovering over Jo's fingers. She meant to say a piece about Jo's perfect bedhead. Or the way her eyes reacted beautifully to light. Or how she commanded attention without even trying. But then, Jo's phone beeped, demanding to be cradled once again.

"Oh, hello, Krissy, 25, Ermita! Finally, someone in the neighborhood," Jo said, an excited grin plastered on her face. Liza's hand retreated, clutching the edge of the table instead.

***

After a few days of exchanging messages, Jo finally scored a date with Krissy, 25, Ermita. They met at a small bar that served craft beers on tap. Mood lights, leather stools, a backlit bar. Only ten people could fit inside. It was nondescript, compared to the multi-colored bar facades that littered this side of Manila. A soft, smooth instrumental filled the dead air between hushed conversations. A couple of loops, and Jo was humming to it, trying to be part of the scene, to belong. She sat by the bartender while waiting.

"For the newbies," the bartender said with a wink as he slid a free shot her way.

"Like, I wouldn't drink that if I were you. Beer is better. Trust." The woman perched on the empty stool next to Jo. She extended a hand, heavy with silver rings. A bundle of thin leather straps wrapped her wrist. They shook hands and exchanged names. Krissy shifted back to call the bartender.

"Two Manila Hipsters," she said, before turning back to Jo.

The bartender slid two mugs of dark beer their way. Jo took a slow sip. She liked the odd taste of it, bitter and fruity at the same time. A pot-bellied man three stools away was eyeing them. He seemed unsettled at the sight of two women without a man hovering around them. He looked like he was thinking of joining them. But a cold, disinterested stare from Jo held him in place.

"First time?" Krissy asked.

"Yes. Strange. I've been in this neighborhood a while, but I've never been here."

"Oh, really? Awesome. Where do you live?"

"Sales. Near the shawarma shack and Mang Larry's."

"Oh, cool! Faura for me. Easier to meet up. Like, if this goes okay, of course."

They did quick work of the basic first-date questions about jobs and weather and families. Neither of them was a serial killer who date-raped or date-murdered people. That was good enough. Jo made it a point to steer clear of conversations about friends. The last thing she wanted to talk about tonight was Liza. It didn't take long for the small talk to run out. Jo waited for Krissy to invite her someplace else.

"Like, I don't know. Do you want to get out of here? My condo's ten minutes away."

"Thought you'd never ask."

What Jo expected to be a routine hookup turned into a sex marathon. It turned out Krissy had quite the stamina. Jo ended up staying the night and going home the following day, her knees shaking like unsettled jelly. Her body throbbed all over. She felt a fever coming on. Jo was an old woman from the waist down. She found Liza sorting a mound of photos on the dining table. Liza had a serious look on her face, creases on her forehead, a tiny frown on her mouth.

"Need help with that?"

"Yeah, actually. But I don't want to bother you. You look tired," Liza said without even looking up from the photos. She was arranging them into neat little piles, for a collage of her recent trip with Christopher. Proof of their loving relationship, Liza's words. For the visa application.

"I don't mind." Jo sat down to help, but not before the classic throw-up, finger-in-mouth gesture.

"OK. So, I've sorted them into three stacks. Cebu, Coron..." Liza gave her the shortest stack. "...and here's the proposal in Laurel. Should be quick and easy. Not as many pictures as the other two."

Great. Of all the piles.

Nevertheless, Jo found a pair of scissors and some glue, and got to work. How happy they looked; Liza beamed like she was sunshine in the flesh. Snip, snip. Here was Christopher, bending down on one knee, while Liza extended her hand and fought back tears. She glued that shot on the center of the paper. Look at Alex and Mang Carding, dressing up for once, with their future son-in-law, by the mango tree in the backyard. The bottle of brandy made it to the shot. Oh, hello, photo of Christopher and Liza smiling at each other.

"So, how was Krissy?"

"She was amazing. My legs are as sore as yours when you lose at the arcade basketball game." Jo leaned back to stretch her legs. She caught Liza shaking her head. "Quite the talker, in bed and off it."

"Been meaning to ask," Liza opened, still poring over the photos, divining the best one for an empty spot in the corner of her collage. "Why the dating romp out of the blue? What, the mistress not enough for you anymore?"

Jo had no answer to that. She stayed silent and kept cutting photos and making them fit into a legal-size bond paper. It wasn't like she could just tell Liza her motivations, this feeling in her chest that she couldn't quite pin down. Most days, it would feel like longing. Then, in a snap, it would easily transform into fear of being left behind. Envy, sometimes, towards Liza's good fortune. Whatever it was, it still had to go. She found that the only way to get over it was to get under people, constantly, like swimming an endless sea. Jo was afraid to stop and entertain that one thought the mistress had sowed in her mind. This was Jo's role in the grand scheme of Liza's American dream. She was the best friend, no more, no less. It was best that way.

"Thank you, by the way."

"For what?"

"For helping me with this. I mean, you're not exactly Christopher's biggest fan."

"But I am yours. You know that."

Liza studied Jo with narrowed eyes, chin propped on an open palm. Her fingers drummed against her cheek, as if trying to see through the muck and chaos of Jo's mind. From the corner of Jo's eye, she saw Liza's gaze soften. It mirrored Jo's own longing. It confused her, the words that followed them more so.

"So sweet. I should have dated you when I had the chance."

"Sorry to burst your bubble, but I don't have a green card."

"There are always exceptions to the rule."

"Ha!" Jo squeaked out.

Jo had to gulp down a glass of water to kill the nervous laughter threatening to escape from her. She rubbed the feverish blush out of her ears. She cleared her throat and pulled her mouth into a frown so it would be harder to smile. This wasn't Jo; this was some ghost walking with her legs, talking with her mouth, making mad leaps with her heart. Jo wiped the glue off her hands with a pot holder. "You know what, I'm going for a smoke."

"I'll come with you." Liza stood up, walking towards the window. She picked up the ashtray, overflowing with days upon days of spent cigarettes, and emptied it into a trash bin.

"No. You know what, I'm going to smoke upstairs. I need some air."

Jo swiped her pack of cigarettes and hurried out the door before Liza could say another word. Once outside, Jo took a breath, one gulp of air to calm her down, and climbed the narrow ladder up the service deck. She welcomed the open space. The noise, the tension didn't reach her here; the heaviness she felt diffused into nothingness. She savored the quiet, holding her breath to stop time.

She wasn't imagining it, was she? Liza was flirting with her. What on earth had brought that on? Jo had no clue. In any case, this was the opposite of the plan. The plan was to get rid of these feelings. The pangs and the heaviness. The flutter and the giddiness. The good and bad. They must be purged from her system. Jo was so wrapped up in her own thoughts that she didn't notice Liza sidling up to her. She gave a start and moved two steps away, leaving Liza reaching for air.

"Is everything OK? You're acting all weird again. Weirder than usual."

"I'm fine," Jo said, crossing her arms across her chest, wearing them like a shield. The circle of cigarette butts surrounding Jo's feet, like a protective hex, begged to differ. "Took a break, is all. Let's go back to your arts and crafts."

Liza caught her wrist and pulled her back. "Let's stay here for a while. The weather's nice."

The evening was cool. The wind whistled through the clothes-lines, sending a white shirt flying past them. They both looked out into the night sky, what little of it they could see between the buildings. Jo had no idea what Liza was thinking of, as much as Liza wasn't privy to the goings-on inside Jo's head. Were they thinking of the same thing? If Jo had asked Liza why she was flirting, would Liza have told her? If Liza had dared to know why Jo was being weird around her, would Jo be willing to spill her guts out? But neither of them dared cross this imaginary line that had come between them. They passed the time breathing in each other's secondhand smoke, stealing glances, keeping within their own little circles. The crescent moon looked exquisite. But Jo didn't seem to notice.

Chapter 11

I t was hard to ignore how the petition had taken over their house and their life. It forced itself in as a third housemate. It interrupted their conversations. It wedged itself under the pillows and into their dreams. It transformed the kitchen into a sea of paper. Post-its, checklists, and notes on backs of receipts. Liza was always on the phone with Christopher, the sweet talk taking a backseat for once.

Pile this up with the stress of Liza's new job. Yes, her new job. One of Liza's gazillion applications had finally pushed through. She found herself manning the cash register at a grocery store. Grocery stores weren't exactly her first choice; matter of fact, she hated them. At least in the department stores, you could move about, follow around a customer if the mood struck. During idle hours, you could stand beside the shelves and talk with the others. A cashier at a grocery store? Not so much. She was chained to the cash register, at the mercy of irate mothers and their wonky pushcarts. Liza had to appease them when a barcode wouldn't take, or when she had to ask the bagger to run to the aisle and check the price. She had to deal with the exasperated huffs and the impatient sighs. There was no idle time at the grocery store. Every second of the day, someone had a need for soap, a toothbrush, a bag of chips, a pack of cotton buds. The never-ending lines stressed her out and left her half-dead by the time her shift ended. Her only consolation? It would be over soon enough. Fingers crossed, this petition should go without a hitch.

"You have got to be kidding me," Jo said, slamming the door behind her. Jo had been out since yesterday on her girlfriend-experience ad. Liza imagined what kind of girlfriend Jo was. Did she win them with her sarcastic remarks and strong side-eye game? Did they laugh at her jokes like Liza did? Was she a good kisser? That last question had Liza snapping back to reality. *Don't go there. Don't go there.*

"Liza! I left you like this, and I come back and you're still... this. It's the fiesta, for fuck's sake! You should be outside!"

It was the feast of San Juan Bautista, which meant the traveling *perya* was in town. Jo ran to the window, watching sadly as the marching band passed by their window. The road was wet with the traditional *basaan*, a commemoration of St. John the Baptist's baptism of Jesus. A group of fire dancers stopped in front of their building. One of the dancers caught her eye, waving an envelope at her.

Jo walked up to Liza and hooked her by the armpits. "That's it. Enough of this never-ending paperwork. Get up. We're going to the perya."

"You go. I have to finish this."

"Oh, come on!" Jo whined, pulling Liza away from this petition that had so consumed her. "That K-1 visa's not going anywhere. Didn't you say you had until Tuesday to send those to Christopher?"

"What time is it?"

"Two p.m."

Liza's stomach grumbled. "Can we at least have lunch first?"

After a quick lunch at Mang Larry's, they were off to the perya. A patch of grassland, sandwiched between a half-finished condominium and a row of rundown eighties hotels, transformed into a brightly lit spectacle. The air was abuzz with bingo numbers, the clack of rusty metal, the cackle of the ghost train and haunted house. The afternoon wasn't burning hot, bringing a sizable crowd to the perya, drawing people to their own favorite vices. For Jo and Liza, it was a shouting match of *cara y cruz* that called to them. They were lucky tonight, winning quite a sum after only a few wagers. They spent their winnings on cotton candy and a round of shoot-the-duck. The loose change that remained, they threw at the squares game, in hopes of scoring a mug or a small pack of Cheese Ring. As they walked from one attraction to another, Liza noticed that Jo's fingers were woven into hers. Liza traced the curve of a smile on her lips.

They lined up at the Ferris wheel, despite Liza's protests. Irrational fear of heights aside, Liza's worries weren't entirely without merit. Anyone would be hard-pressed to trust the rusty hinges and an open carriage that swung in such a steep arc. Jo somehow convinced her to ride along. Wheel of death, she called it. Liza unraveled at the first go-around. Her nails dug into Jo's arms. Their carriage creaked at every swing, at three stories high. They went around so fast, their stomachs pounded against their backs. Peals of thrilled laughter mixed with horrified screams of "Please, *manong*! Stop!"

Pale and cold as a corpse, Liza held on to the railings as they exited. She bent over, trying hard not to hurl the cotton candy she'd had earlier. "Joanna, please don't tell me we're hitting the haunted house next. You're trying too hard to give me a heart attack."

"Uhh...," Jo replied, hands squirming inside her pockets, weight shifting from one leg to the other. "No, you know what. You're right. We've had our fun. I think I scared you too much with the Ferris wheel. Let's head back home."

Liza perked her head up, sensing something afoot. She blocked Jo's way, held her by the hips, and sniffed around her. "Is that the stench of fear I'm smelling? On you? The fearless Joanna Suarez, afraid of fake ghosts?"

"Me? Afraid of ghosts? Of course not. Just that—that GFE ad was a bitch, so demanding! I'm tired. Ready to hit the bed."

"Do you think I can't tell when you're lying?"

Jo could have been half-dead for all Liza cared. She would not be denied her revenge. She pulled Jo away from the exit, past the gambling stalls and bingo tables, and dragged her all the way to the darkest corner of the grounds. The haunted house was a lonely fixture in the back, with a gaping clown mouth serving as the entrance. Two red lightbulbs served as eyes, blinking in time with the looping evil-laugh track. Dusty black curtains hid the attraction—or, as Jo would put it, the needless horror—from plain sight.

***

Liza ran right into it, while Jo took her time. Her steps were small, slow, hesitant. The gate was locked now; the only exit was on the other side. She could back out. She was twenty-eight—a grown-ass adult, for crying out loud. She wasn't some pimply teenage girl forced to complete a dare for the sake of friendship. But then again, Jo thought it only seemed fair. She got her kicks playing on Liza's fear of heights. It was only right that Liza got her licks, too. Jo pumped her fists, braced herself, parted the curtains, and entered. In the grayish darkness, it was difficult to see. Jo couldn't pick out Liza from the crowd in front of her. She had a feeling Liza had lost her on purpose. Only halfway through, Jo's insides were already swimming in adrenaline and terror. Her throat was hoarse from screaming. She jumped when a stray plastic bag brushed the back of her neck. She almost punched a lady in white lunging at her from a hidden door. She could hear the titters of a group of teenagers. Signs of life. Strangely, without Liza, she didn't feel safe. Only when she saw the light of the exit—the carousel peeked every time the black curtain was raised—did she feel the slightest sense of relief. She was hurrying towards it, when a bone-yellow hand pulled her into another secret door. Jo screamed, saving her best shriek for last, only to find that it was Liza playing a prank on her.

"I will—I swear to god, Liza. I will get you for this," Jo hissed, her threat drowned by Liza's incessant cackles.

"Saw you with that werewolf. Man, he got you good." Liza flailed her arms and mouthed a silent scream, mimicking Jo's terror. "The white lady, too. I mean, she came at you as slow as a snail on a bad day!"

"And that plastic bag!"

"And the bat from the ceiling! Oh, Jo!"

Rough and tough and wild-haired Jo feared people in costume, fake hair, and makeup. Liza milked this nugget of discovery for all its worth, while Jo sulked with her arms folded across her chest. Jo waited for the prank to run its course. In ten minutes that felt like forever, Liza's boisterous cackles started fading into soft, breathless huffs. Then silence, save for their breathing. Jo became aware of how small the space was, and how close they were to each other. Jo was pressed up against a GI sheet, while Liza's hands gripped Jo's shoulders for balance. Her thigh wedged itself between Jo's legs, her knee almost

89

ramming Jo in the groin. Jo's left hand curled around the hem of Liza's shirt. Neither one of them attempted to shift, to break free from this body lock. Neither of them segued to "Hey, let's get some of that weird-tasting pink popcorn!" or "Let's try bingo this time!" Jo held her breath, waiting for this moment to play itself out.

It must have been the cramped space that forced Liza to shift. Or Jo's hand brushing against a patch of ticklish skin on Liza's waist. Or the moonlight creeping through the cracks on the roof. Liza moved, but not to shift away. She wasn't trying to break free. The pink popcorn was a world away. Even the music and the screams and the humming of motors that powered the rides became as far from her ears as a half-forgotten dream. Somewhere, a door slammed. Somewhere, a child screamed in terror. Somewhere, some lucky fella won it all at B6. Here, though, here, Liza pressed her lips against Jo's. Here, under slats of the ever-changing lights of the perya, they kissed. The kiss was the night, the world, and the universe. It was fireworks. It was "Bingo!" and shrill shrieks towards the gods of fortune. It was the evil cackles, mocking them, privy to all that they kept hidden. It was the whisper behind the door, followed by receding footsteps.

Maybe we shouldn't do this. This is scary as fuck, and I want out.

Jo dipped her hand under Liza's shirt. Liza flinched and trembled, like a compass readjusting its bearings, circling back to its true north. Jo was a tangent, not the destination. Without a word, Liza shifted away, swinging the door open, walking towards the exit, out into the night. Every breath seemed to have formed a cloud around her, cloying and much too warm. She watched the Ferris wheel go round and round. The screams weren't as bad as the pounding in her ears, the imaginary vise grip squeezing her lungs into small, pathetic sacs, her feet losing all sense of direction. Liza would rather free fall ten thousand times over than face the fear of what had already changed.

Chapter 12

This was awkward. How were they going to sleep in the same bed after that kiss? Jo wished she hadn't thrown out the double deck. That could have provided the separation they needed, while still being in the same space. Should she kick her out? That was too harsh a response. Jo was still reeling from the kiss, but she needed answers. Answers which she would most likely never get. Still, she had to try. She caught up with Liza at the entrance.

"Why did you kiss me?"

"Look, Jo. Whatever it was, it can't happen again."

"You don't even want to talk about it?"

"What is there to talk about?"

Jo was tired of this. Tired of pretending that nothing had changed between them. But Liza didn't seem to care. The petition was more important. Christopher was more important. Jo didn't matter.

"Fine. You want to pretend nothing happened? Two can play that game," Jo snapped.

"I'm moving out. It's better if we—"

"You know what, do what you want. I don't care. You obviously don't." She walked away from Liza, towards a drink or two, a fuck or two.

Liza made good on her threat and moved out in two days, like she said she would. Jo didn't help her this time. She let Liza haul out her stuff on her own. Jo continued her romp, doubling up on her dates and ads. She hunted the weekend bookings to nearby provinces. She bit the bullet on a Baguio-Tagaytay-Batangas casual weekend leg. Anything to not be left alone with her thoughts. Everything was going well until she crashed into Lara, 39, Makati. On the surface, she fit right smack into Jo's target demographic. Neat little bob. Moisturizer and lipstick and done. Body-hugging dress and gold bangles. Lara looked like she had heard all the half-truth pleasantries and didn't bother with them as much. *She wants you, she'll let you know.* And, there was no mistaking it: Lara wanted her. There was no mistaking the way Jo's name rolled like a sweet treat off her tongue. There was no mistaking how close Lara leaned into her. There was no mistaking how her eyes crept up and down Jo's legs. All the signs pointed to the right direction until Jo made a passing anecdote about a former ad.

"He had very specific requests, but nothing I can't handle. Black dresses. Pale pink lipstick. Did I mind having my hair in a half-pony and hairpins? Did I object to wearing wire-rim glasses?" She took a sip of her overpriced beer. Paying two hundred pesos for a Pale Pilsen was a travesty. But up until that point, the price was worth Lara's company. She was enjoying herself.

"It was all good. I think he wanted to go back to the things his wife used to do for him when they were younger. If you look at it from another angle, kinda sweet, don't you think? And the tips! My god, I lived off those tips for a year! I think he's dead now, bless him."

"Wait, you get paid to have sex?" Lara asked, a perplexed

look on her face, digesting what the anecdote revealed about Jo. Jo had her in a spell up until that point. Judging by the sharp tone in her voice, the date was hurtling towards an irrevocable and disastrous ending.

When Jo refused to offer apologies, the confusion on Lara's face turned into disgust. Strange how humans unravel. One moment, she was ready to take Jo home. After that story, she was leaning away, calling the bartender for the bill. She shook off Jo's presence like one would shoo flies. She settled her tab in a hurry. On her way out, Lara threw Jo a look that would stop anyone cold. It was as if Jo had betrayed her confidence, taken advantage of her trust, deceived her into spending the night. A complete waste of time.

Jo had been on the losing end of this double standard countless times. Nobody batted an eyelash when an upper-class lady sauntered into a bar and flirted with a stranger. *Leave her alone; she's modern and progressive and liberated.* Jo did the exact same thing, except that she got paid. Funny thing about tonight, she wasn't even intent on getting paid. She wanted to have a good time, plain and simple as that. Perhaps she should feel a tinge of regret about losing a conquest. But hypocrites didn't make for very enjoyable pursuits.

It was still only eight p.m. The date had ended bright and early compared to the ones Jo had of late. It was easy to swipe for a substitute; she could hook a replacement within minutes. She could still save the night. But Lara had killed the mood. She would rather go home and leave it all to hell.

Jo always squared up in these kinds of encounters, ready to fight, making sure she stood up for herself. She did not warrant or deserve disgust. They had no right to tell her what she could and couldn't do with her body. True, there were some damning circumstances that led her here. True, she carried a trail of bad decisions around like a cape. But sex work was a choice she made of her own will, and she would never be ashamed of it. There were days like this, though, when the conviction wavered a little bit. Days when Jo got to thinking that maybe they were right to feel repulsed. She deserved to get walked out on. She wasn't a worthy conquest because she could be bought.

At home, Jo walked straight to bed and curled up into a tiny ball. She squeezed into a corner, burying herself under a fort of sheets and pillows. Her fingers hovered over her phone. There was one person she could call to fix the wounds cut open by a look, a condescending question, a serving of hasty judgment. She needed the familiar to get through this. She needed the familiar to erase a stranger's impression. Days like this, she needed the familiar to say she was beautiful and brilliant and good.

At the back of Jo's heart, she knew they were better off apart. She knew that. Liza knew that. She had to move on from that kiss, from the aftermath, from these more-than-friendly intentions. Pretend it didn't happen. Pretend they were just friends, like always. If only it were that easy. Pretending took an admirable level of self-control, something that Jo didn't have.

She dialed Liza's number and waited.

***

"I've submitted the petition!" Christopher's voice boomed all around Liza's new place. Good thing her roommates were out. He unfolded a piece of paper and aimed the camera at the stamp of approval.

"That's good news," Liza said, her words an ill match to the monotone in her voice. She might as well have been an automated phone operator in a customer service hotline. Or this one concierge at the mall she worked in. Such a scintillating example of cheerfulness.

Liza remembered dancing in the rain in Coron. She remembered walking with Christopher in Cebu until her feet grew blisters. She remembered the way Christopher held her every single time they made love. She thought of Christopher's relationship with Alex. Alex listened to him. In the space of a weekend, Christopher had fared better at figuring out Alex than Liza had in years. She felt guilty about not being excited enough for this bit of news.

"Didn't you say Jo helped you out with that one?"

Jo. In the space of a second, Liza's mind jumped to the night at the haunted house. She bit her lip, licked it clean. How come she could still taste Jo weeks after that kiss? How come a slight, trembling ache traveled up and down her spine, nerves coming alive all at once? How come the mere memory of it made her pulse pound with excitement? Christopher was talking about interview schedules and document fees. His voice felt as if it were behind a door.

Door, a secret door, Liza imagined. The haunted house. With Jo pressed against her.

Focus.

Christopher kept snapping his fingers, trying to catch Liza's attention. She didn't realize how long she had been spacing out. "Babe, I heard that appointments fill up really quick there. So, once the application gets routed to Manila, I need you to schedule an interview ASAP. Should I send money for the fees?"

"Sure."

"Is everything all right? You seem out of it," Christopher asked, his shoulders tensing up. He shifted closer, spilling out of the screen at times. He rubbed his hand against day-old stubble. His eyes narrowed.

"Can we talk about something else? This petition is making me nervous."

Christopher obliged and talked about the weather instead. It was summer there, so he had been spending more time outdoors. His bare torso was a shade darker than usual. He had been scavenging for driftwood, finding the right pieces for his hobby projects. The business was doing good, too. He'd recently got involved in a tiny house project for a newlywed two streets down. Liza nodded along, but her mind was elsewhere. These things used to interest Liza. Now, they tasted like sickbed crackers laid to melt in her mouth.

"Well, I have to go now."

"Bye, babe."

"Give my regards to Nanay. And, tell Alex I bought him new Jordans! And Mac and *Tatay*, I hope they are well. And, babe, please try not to worry about the petition too much. It will be fine. We will be fine." Christopher gave her that shy smile, baring the gentle soul underneath all the muscle. "I cannot wait for you to be here. With me.

"I love you," he added.

"I —," Liza started to say before the line went dead. She didn't bother calling back.

A few months ago, she would have been gushing with the sweetest words for him. She would have been as red as a tomato, the way he made her blush. The prospect of living in America with the man she loved should feel like a fairy tale. But when she kissed Jo, she'd felt something inside her unravel. This strange and new intimacy between them scared her into leaving, and had her wondering where all this could have started. Her mind would go back to the perya, back to that talk at the Appliance

Center, back to sleeping on the same bed, to all their Mang Larry's dates, to the very day Liza heard her sing. *"Piano in the Dark"*, she remembered. Had it been sleeping inside her all along?

Focus.

She looked at the time. It would just be past dinner in Laurel. Her mother would be in the kitchen, poring over today's profits at the market, a small cup of herbal tea by her elbow. Mang Carding would either be punch drunk or reading yesterday's tabloids. Alex would be at home, holed up in his room, if it had been a good day. Liza hoped for a good day.

"What made you call, *anak*?"

"Nothing, 'Nay. I just wanted to hear your voice."

"Is everything all right?"

"I just miss you. That's all."

"Come home soon," her mother pleaded. "Mac misses you."

"I will, 'Nay," Liza replied. "Christopher submitted the petition already. Now, all we do is wait. Four to six months."

Liza heard Mang Carding's voice in the background, and a scrambling towards the kitchen.

"What? What did she say? Are we going to the, to the America now?"

"No one's going to the U.S. yet," Liza explained.

"Wow! But the petition is in the works, no?" Liza had never heard Mang Carding this excited in years. "Wow. You did good, anak. You did good marrying Christopher. Wow. Living in America!"

It turned out to be more than a good day. Not only was Alex in the house, he was out of his room and playing with Mac. He, too, sent his congratulations.

"Nanay said there's a chance we could live there with you?"

Alex said. "She said if I finish college, it ups the chances? Or is she just shitting me?"

"Nothing's a done deal yet. But I'll try my best to get you there, Alex," Liza said. "Oh, before I forget, Christopher bought you a new pair of Jordans."

"Which one?"

"I have no idea," Liza laughed. "They all look the same to me."

Alex gasped. "You did not just say that!"

They shared a laugh, a rare commodity these days between the two of them. Alex sighed, the lilt of hope drowning the usual languor in his voice. "Thank you, *Ate*. And, congratulations!"

"Don't congratulate me yet."

It was the kind of call she needed to get her head straight. It reminded Liza why she'd held on to this dream for so long, tooth and nail and self-esteem all in. She fought hard to get here. Here, in a studio apartment shared with three others. Here, an interview away from her American fiancé, from a 500-square-meter bungalow with a pool out back. Here, with her family catching her up on stories around town, sharing a glimpse of the future that lay ahead. They were the reason, the straight and narrow for when she went astray.

Focus.

Her phone rang, the name on the screen making her heart leap. She let it ring longer than usual, praying it would stop, wishing it wouldn't.

"Jo? What's up? Is something wrong?"

So much for focus. So much for the straight and narrow. So much for the future. She smoothed her polo shirt, tied her hair back in a ponytail, picked up the pink hoodie hanging from the bedpost, and ran out the door.

***

"I know you're still mad, so I brought gifts." Liza raised a clear plastic bag, bearing a tub of Double Dutch and six cans of Red Horse. Jo's surefire pick-me-uppers. Jo ignored the gifts and held Liza instead.

"There, there," Liza said, returning the embrace, her free hand gentle on Jo's back. "Come on, this ice cream won't eat itself."

"Let's go upstairs."

Up at the service deck, they staked a spot under an old and rusty water tank. Between swigs of beer, they recalled drunken nights and the unexplained mornings they left in their wake. Waking up in each other's clothes. Liza sleeping by an open refrigerator, clutching a bowl of rice. Jo's penchant for throwing up in the weirdest places. She hid her face at the memory of that one night behind the carabao at Quirino Grandstand.

"Are you feeling better?" Liza asked.

"A little bit. I still feel so ugly."

"You're beautiful, you know that," Liza said, laying a hand on Jo's cheek. Her touch burned like ice, but Jo didn't mind. Jo held on to Liza's words like driftwood on a raging sea. "No Forbes Park bitch can tell you otherwise."

"You're beautiful," Liza repeated.

Jo set down her bowl and looked at Liza. There was a question she had been meaning to ask. Jo tried to pretend the kiss hadn't happened. She tried to forget the feel of Liza's skin on hers. She tried to numb the taste of her mouth, the dark haze in her eyes when Liza leaned against her inside behind that door in the haunted house.

"Liza..." Jo puffed her cheeks and exhaled slowly. She drew circles on Liza's wrist, surprised at not meeting any resistance.

"Why did you kiss me at the haunted house?"

"I love Christopher, Jo," Liza said.

"Okay. But that's not what I'm asking."

Liza withdrew her wrist, looked up at the water tank, and banged her head against the wall. "I don't know, Jo, okay? I just did. I know I shouldn't have kissed you. But, my god, I wanted to so much. Honest, I don't know what's going on with me. I look at my ring, I talk to Christopher, but it's background noise in my head. All I can think of is that kiss. I can't stop thinking about it. I feel sick in the stomach with guilt for acting like this. I promised myself I'd stay away. This wasn't the plan. But, one call from you, and I break that promise. Seeing your face again, and it all goes away. The world, my world, shrinks to this. Ice cream. And beer. And you."

Jo kissed her before she could say anything more. It was a light kiss, lingering at Liza's bottom lip, testing the waters before committing to anything more. Again, Liza offered no resistance. Instead, the resistance came from Jo's own mind. *Don't do this*, a tiny voice inside her seemed to say. *Don't say it.* She'd never said those words, not like this, not for the way she felt about Liza right now. But what was she going to do when the weight of the words was lodged in her throat, struggling to gush out? Saying it out loud was too great a leap. So, she did the next best thing. She whispered it unto Liza's mouth, slowly parting to kiss her again.

"I love you."

The thoughts in Jo's head swerved and burned and merged, like cars and jeepneys in Divisoria. What does this mean? What happens after this? Should I be doing this? She reminded herself once again of the plan—her own plan. It was the right thing to do for her sanity. But what was sanity when Liza's breath was on her neck, followed by the wet warmth of her lips? What was right and wrong when Liza's thumb traced Jo's ribs like she was trying to memorize the grooves of her body? Why did the right thing sound so unappealing? What about Christopher?

What about him? He was half a world away.

Liza had a look about her, one Jo was only too familiar with. It was that look when an ad had had enough of the small talk and light pecking. It was that look that sent Jo undressing in a hurry. It was that look that meant the next fifteen minutes, at least, would be a blur of skin, sweat, and unpleasant sounds. Imagining what could happen had Jo gasping for air. Whether it was dread or excitement, she couldn't tell for sure.

"Tell me where to go," Jo breathed.

"Downstairs. Bed. Now."

They clambered down the rusty steps, ignoring the muffled complaints of the neighbors. Back down, Jo found herself wedged between Liza and the door. *Don't open the door*, that tiny voice of reason ordered. The knob weighed a ton in Jo's hand. There was a way out of this. *Buy a pack of cigarettes, say you've run out. Walk it out. Walk the storm of emotions inside you until it's nothing but a harmless white cloud on a blue sky.* But it was exhausting trying to run away from this. Jo was done thinking her way out. Let them stumble into this uncertainty. Let the pieces fall where they may.

Jo twisted the doorknob.

Chapter 13

J o once had an ad who was the most clueless virgin ever. He didn't bring a condom even when Jo told him to. When she gave him one, he looked at it like some plastic balloon toy that he needed to let float out the window. His kisses were too eager, intent on knocking out Jo's teeth. When he tasted her mouth, his tongue slithered like a windshield wiper. So lost was he in this tide of new sensations that Jo had to steer him from start to finish. He was a puppet, a plaything brought to life by Jo's skilled hands. The ending didn't take too long. He was gone in sixty seconds.

It didn't matter if the ad was good, bad, ugly, terrible, clueless, know-it-all. Jo's main pursuit was to please. She was very good at pleasing people, improving with every encounter. These taught her every ticklish bone in the body. She knew the basics of every imaginable fetish. Sucking feet, tentacle porn, golden showers. Name it. She knew better, she knew a lot. So it was only natural for Jo to direct Liza like she did that poor little clueless ad. The goal was to make this last longer than a quick minute. She kissed Liza until her lungs begged for air. She followed the heat from every blushing patch of skin, and tasted it until her tongue grew numb and raw. She welcomed the burning ache in her arm, the stiffness of her right wrist. She finished strong and well, with Liza exploding in discontinuous jerks underneath her.

It was as good a performance as any. The contented hum on Liza's lips told as much. Jo waited for her own feeling of satisfaction to creep in. It did come, but barely and not enough. Jo felt incomplete and unsatisfied, despite all the telltale signs of a job well done. Liza was calling her name, gentle, soft, like a voice in a dream. She responded with a weak "Yes?" and realized that her free hand still had Liza by the wrists.

"Let me," Liza whispered. It was as simple a command as any, shorter than most safe words Jo had to memorize. *Let me.* It was less complicated than most requests she'd had to fulfill.

Let me, Liza said, and so Jo did. By repetition, Jo had conditioned herself to please, give, take control. This time, though, she loosened her grip and let go. As Liza trailed kisses down her neck and chest, stopping to feel her heartbeat, Jo found herself breaking from the chains of habit. At the mercy of Liza's bidding, Jo rediscovered satisfaction. She couldn't stifle the moan that rose up her throat as Liza's fingers brushed against her side. She should be ticklish, but it wasn't laughter pooling and swirling inside her. When Liza closed her eyes, Jo wondered if Liza was thinking of her. The hope that Liza was thinking of her made her every nerve come alive. Liza's hand slipped between her thighs, fingers tentative, taking their sweet time. The slow burn was fucking with Jo's patience. When Liza quickened her pace, more sure now, steadier, Jo's heart was about ready to leap out of her chest. All this activity, all at once, made Jo want to burst into tears. Was this what love felt like? Like a tangled live wire, sparking, spreading, exploding at every touch?

"I want to taste you," Liza said with bated breath.

Old habits reared their ugly heads, firing commands left and right. Say no. Roll her over. Fuck the living daylights out of her. Give. Please. Take control. All the old rules changed with those two words. *Let me.* Jo took a sharp breath and nodded before she could change her mind. *Let me*, Liza said. So, Jo let her.

Jo let Liza introduce her to these fearfully new and strange feelings. She let Liza pick at her pretenses, her defenses, like peeling old paint off a wall, revealing the tired colors beneath. Soft and wet licks met fast and hard thrusts, until Jo couldn't tell which was which anymore. Her body was ripping apart, coming undone. It was rearranging not exactly into order, but into a different state of chaos. The chaos and order, the conflict and peace, the sureness and uncertainty, was Liza. Jo sank to the bed, exhausted and numbed by this transformation. She knew—how exactly, she didn't know —that she wasn't the same person anymore.

It was a quarter past one, but Jo still couldn't buy sleep. Her senses were far from tired. Every color, sound, taste, scent, and feeling was fresh and sharp. She was a newborn adjusting to the world. She caught every sliver of light creeping through the window. The faint smell of Liza's shampoo, now tinged with salt and sweat, mixed with her every breath. She was aware of every tick-tock of the wall clock. She felt the weight of Liza on her arm. A part of her wanted to wriggle free. *It's not too late to run*, came the chants from her old self.

Jo was a proud woman. She disguised it in off-handed retorts and half-jokes, but she was proud of having made it this far. She wore her struggles close to her chest, like a soldier with her medals. Her triumphs, small or big, were her armor. She could always work her way out of trouble. She could get what she wanted without anybody's help. She wasn't one to beg or grovel or wish or plead. Until now.

"Choose me," Jo whispered, as she brushed the wisps of hair from Liza's eyes.

In her dreams, Liza did exactly that. The setting shifted to different towns and cities, houses and cottages, mountainsides and sandy shores. But the ending was the same. Liza chose her over and over again. Jo didn't have to beg. Jo didn't have to say it out loud. She was enough to change her mind.

But dreams and reality seldom aligned. The morning after was no exception. Jo rolled over and found the good side of the bed empty. She didn't know how long Liza had been sitting in the kitchen, with all her clothes on. She hadn't left in the middle of the night, had made it through daylight. But judging by the apologetic look in Liza's eyes, she might as well have. At the prospect of losing Liza, the words rallied in Jo's mind. She couldn't give this up. *Tell her to stay. Tell her to choose you. Tell her, tell her, tell her that you love her. Tell her that you are enough, with or without the green card. Even if it were never more than this, it would always be enough. Say something. Tell her.* But in the short distance between mind and mouth, heart and mind, the words got lost in translation.

Please stay. "You're leaving, aren't you?"

"I can't do this, Jo."

Fight for me. "What do you mean you can't do this?"

"I can't do this with you. Please, Jo, try to understand."

Choose me. "Understand what? That you love me and you're marrying someone else? How could I possibly understand that?"

"Because you know me better than anyone, Jo. I'm marrying Christopher and leaving for the U.S. The U.S.! You know this is a dream come true."

You are what I dream of. "Is that your dream still?"

One blink and she would have missed the slight shake of Liza's head. The softest no was enough to give Jo the tiniest bit of hope.

We could have a life together. "Is that the life you want?"

"It's the life they need."

Stay, please. "Stay, please," Jo said, mind and mouth agreeing at last.

Liza's voice cracked, fighting back tears. From the edge of the bed, Jo watched the last five years unravel in front of her. There was no going back from this. No pretending nothing happened. No ignoring the mess of a love spilled. This was the end, plain and blunt and crude and simple. All clichés, all the songs about love, all the words spoken and written in its honor: didn't they all say love wins? Love is the most powerful thing? Love moves mountains? Jo scoffed at the utter stupidity of it all. So much for love, when she felt like the mountain was inside her chest, pinning her down, choking her.

Liza knelt in front of her. Liza's hands were rough, her grip squeezing what little fight remained inside Jo. "If I were the only one who mattered, if I were free to choose, you know I would stay. Hell, I would run away with you. To the ends of the world, if you want me to. I would figure this life out with you. Gladly. A simple life with you would be enough. But, it's not just me, Jo, do you understand? There's Nanay and Mac and Alex. Even Papa. It's never just me. Will never be just me. I am their ticket to a better life."

"Liza, you don't have to be if you don't want to."

"But wanting has nothing to do with it. I have to because nobody else will. They matter more than me. More than you, Jo. There will never be a world that they don't come first. That's why I'm giving you up. That's why I'm marrying Christopher.

That's why this has to end."

"At least, tell me you love him."

"He has a guest house ready for them. They're going to live there. It may take a long time. But he wants them there. He wants to give them that life."

"Tell me you love him."

"Mac is in love with the inflatable pool. Remember that? The one in Christopher's backyard?"

"Tell me you love him, so I can just forget you. This."

Liza had run out of excuses. The silence spoke for her. It made little sense for Jo to fight a losing battle. She would never win against family. She was an outsider, no matter how she spun it. It didn't matter that they'd once shared a bed, a closet, highs that were always gone too soon and hellish lows that felt like eternities. She had lost. What a fool she was to give this love a chance when it had been a losing affair from the start.

Liza stood up and walked to the door, caught between staying and leaving, tied down by the tears in Jo's eyes. They could go on like this, talk their ears off, but Jo knew she still couldn't make Liza stay. Liza wouldn't choose her either way. The merciful thing was to release Liza from this limbo, relieve her of the guilt, get out of the way as Liza's childhood dreams hurtled to fruition.

Wiping the tears from her eyes, Jo walked towards Liza and cupped her cheeks. She held her face, branding every groove, every scar, every mole to memory. Jo kissed her and took in the salt in her tears, the smoke in her mouth, the sigh in her breath. This was how goodbyes tasted; she wouldn't be able to remember anything else.

"Someday, I hope you realize that you matter, too."

She twisted the doorknob.

She swung the door wide open.
She let her go.

Chapter 14

That first night, she waited for Liza to come back. She left the chain and the bolts undone, so Liza could slip inside and they could sleep in the same bed like always. *One night*, Jo bargained. She would mourn for one more night. Bargaining with a broken heart never worked for anybody. The sleepless hours soon became the norm. The days wore on and began to darken into a black hole of waiting for her phone to ring. She didn't know if she wanted to set fire to her memories of Liza or build a dictionary of apologies and I love yous and change your mind, please.

I can give you the life you want. I love you. Please come back.

Backspace, backspace, backspace.

She couldn't stay cooped up like this, stalking the street below for a shock of Liza's faded highlights. Or that ratty backpack. Or the same balikbayan boxes she'd lugged in here the last endo. Jo needed to not exist for a while, pretend that she was fine. She walked out into the early evening, up to the street corner and hailed a taxi. A drive around Makati should provide a moment's escape. There was surely a bar in there dark and obscure enough to hole in and hide. This life, this fucked-up life that had been spinning madly on for twenty-eight years had thrown her off-orbit yet again. After a few lengthy loops around Greenbelt, Jo stumbled upon her dark and obscure bar. The driver asked her for a tip, citing this and that inconvenience, wasting his gas and time and all that. She gave him her middle finger.

Perhaps, her mind was too distracted to recognize that this was the same place that Lara, 39, Makati did a spectacle of shaming her. When it finally hit her, the memory piled up the hurt onto Jo's already-battered heart. That should have been a warning sign, an impetus to go out and look for another place to perch. But the barstool was soft and she was already in the middle of a stiff drink. Whiskey for all her troubles.

"Another one, please?"

Time passed her by, half-hours marked with the bartender setting glass upon glass in front of her. The alcohol was starting to kick in when a stranger thought it was a good idea to invade her personal space. He was a brute of a man, reeking of onions and beer left to stew in the sun. He clapped her on the back with a hand that was equal parts hair and flesh. He claimed to be a former client. Jo didn't remember him at all. Fuck, she would remember servicing a werewolf.

"Hey, I remember you." His onion breath made her whiskey-induced headache worse. "How's the going rate these days? Or, should I say coming?"

He clapped her on the back again. Jo could swear her spine cracked at the force. "Say, could you help a brother out? Three pops ought to do it for me tonight."

"I'm off the clock, sorry."

"Come on, I'll double the rate."

"No, dude, go away. I'm off the clock," Jo said, swiveling her stool away.

Like every other man who misconstrued a hard no as the start of a conversation, he pressed his agenda. He leaned forward against Jo's back and dipped down a hand to cup her breast. She wasn't in the mood for this. Never in the mood for unsolicited, totally not-consensual fondling.

"What part of 'off the clock' don't you understand?"

Jo swiped the hand off her chest and punched him in the face. If he didn't think a girl could throw a cold left hook, she was much obliged to correct that assumption. The man staggered to a nearby table, stumbling onto another girl's lap. The girl let out a yelp, which had her boyfriend shoving Mr. Werewolf back towards Jo. One moment, Jo was putting her drink down. The next, she was on the ground, a throbbing pain registering somewhere on the left side of her face.

The scene became a blur of black-shirted bouncers and muted expletives. A drink was thrown in somebody's face. Groggy as all hell, she stood up and snuck a hard knee to the man's groin. Despite his alleged VIP status, Mr. Werewolf got kicked out of the bar. It was a victory. A small one, but a victory nonetheless. She wanted to celebrate, but the stiff drink did not go well with the bloody eyebrow and the weird stares. Jo had killed the vibe; this was supposed to be a quiet and fancy kind of place, and Jo had ruined it by causing a scene. This party was better off resumed somewhere else. As Jo exited the bar, she took stock of herself in the mirror. The little fucker did her eye good, but she'd had worse. Her fingers hovered over Liza's last text message. She held her breath and dialed a number.

"Can you pick me up, please?" She looked around for a street sign. "Dela Rosa. Greenbelt, the side with the museum cafe."

No amount of wine or whiskey could numb this ache. Tears stung her eyes at how helpless and stupid she felt. How had it come to this? How did she go from dancing through life to getting a black eye in a bar brawl? She wiped fresh tears with the back of her hand. Her knuckles held a faint stain of rusty red.

That gray Mercedes C-Class took its time getting here, but Jo had never been happier seeing it pull over in front of her. As it approached, she sniffed and choked back any sign of weakness. She stood up straighter, shoulders tensed, chest high and proud. She swept back the curls of her hair and tied them up in a loose bun. The mistress rolled down her window halfway through. She took stock of Jo's swollen eye, the dried blood, the bleary makeup, the haphazard ponytail.

"Take me away, please? I need to disappear for a couple days."

"The Liza thing didn't work out, I take it."

Jo could only nod, her lips quivering.

The passenger door clicked open. "Get in."

It must have been the leather seat giving in to her weight. Or the rhythmic hum of the engine. It could have been plain exhaustion or the soothing brush of the mistress's hand on hers. Whatever it was, it made Jo fall into a deep sleep and kept her there throughout the trip. She woke up to a darkness made eerie by the glow of headlights. She could make out trees in the distance. A cottage loomed outside her window.

"Where are we?"

"You said you needed to disappear."

The click of the car door startled Jo. The mistress let go of the steering wheel and put the engine to rest. A scratching noise reached Jo's ears. Crickets? Exactly how far were they from the closest sign of civilization?

"This is disappearing, my dear."

The cottage was larger than it looked. The scarcity of furniture lent the illusion of an even bigger space. Every piece looked like it was worth two lifetimes and half her soul. She sat on the floor, leaning against the gray-green couch. The mistress came back with a bag of ice and a tray of fresh-brewed coffee. She laid down the tray and rubbed the ice bag around Jo's eye.

Water dripped down the side of Jo's face. The mistress was as calm and composed as ever. They stared at each other, both broken but too proud to admit it. They shared this incurable need for what they couldn't have. So they went ahead and bit the pill that always worked. They pushed each other down the carpet, fought over who gets to be the top first, and fucked it all away. The pain, the fear, the misery.

"He's never fucked me on this carpet before," the mistress said as they lay naked, staring at the ceiling. Jo gently pressed a finger over her eye. It started to hurt again.

"Does he even do anything for you anymore?"

"Well, he did buy me this cottage."

"We could live like this, you know. In a shoebox far away from here."

The mistress pointed a slim, bejeweled finger upwards. "How long do you think until I hate you for taking me away from that lovely chandelier? And that Mercedes outside. And these diamond earrings. How long until you hate me for being second best?"

"We could be happy."

"Jo, I'm good for an escape every now and then. That's all we have." The mistress held her tight. It was a prayer into the night, a wish for better days ahead. "Whatever this is, whatever Liza did to you, you have to survive it. Find your happiness, my dear. One you don't have to disappear from."

Chapter 15

Did a three-month trip to the North count as disappearing? It wasn't disappearing, was it, if she drifted for a while in search for a place to land?

Jo had been toying with this idea for many a night, lying in bed, holding on to moments of clarity until she slipped into a black hole her mind could not escape from. Where she once sought drama and excitement, a life in Technicolor, she now found a silent film in grainy black and white. The ads still paid well, but Jo found it harder and harder to bother herself with servicing the unfucked. The buildings looked gray, the roads dirty, the night terribly unappetizing and dull. She needed to get away for a while. La Union. Benguet. Sagada. Cagayan. Batanes, if the weather permitted. Who knows, she might even get away for good. Consider these three months of backpacking and odd jobs a test drive. She gave a part of her savings to cover rent until she came back. Until then, she didn't want to decide.

***

Jo couldn't decide on this booking, thanks to a fever that just wouldn't go away. After flip-flopping for half the day, she decided to push through with it. It was a low-hanging fruit of an arrangement anyway. Escort for hire, at one of those obnoxious fratboy reunions. No sex. She only needed to show up in a tight bandage dress and sleek updo. The ad was a fifty-something, smooth-faced, rosy-cheeked CEO of a local shipping line. He hired Jo so he could look the part of an eligible bachelor. He had the looks that could make anyone swoon and kneel, no questions asked, but he was too busy to date. It was all ships with him; if he could bring an oil tanker with him on these events, he probably would.

Traffic, as usual, was at a standstill. To pass the time, Jo meant to ask if the ad had paid for escort service before. But the restraint wearing down the ad's lips had Jo biting her tongue. She kept her peace, as the chauffeur-driven Audi jogged to a two-story loft bar in the upscale part of Taguig. As soon as they arrived, all hope of brokering a conversation with her ad was dashed. A carousel of dinosaurs, also known as dirty old men, occupied him. Jo needed to work it, too. There were handshakes to be given, men to be politely smiled at, dressed-up Fita crackers to be eaten. There was dead air to get rid of when anyone started a lengthy, uneventful chat with her. Bed death, home improvements, and cars and such.

"Sorry. Got held up by some grand masters. Are you feeling all right?" her ad asked. He swooped two glasses of champagne from a passing waiter, and gave one to Jo.

Jo was about to respond and catch him up on all the frat gossip when an old man with a sorry comb-over approached them. He groped a rheumatic hand around Jo's waist, crossing dangerous territory down her thigh. Strike one. Jo responded by shifting away. Subtle. Polite.

"You are so pretty. Quite a looker you got in your harem, Lopez." He leered at Jo, smacking his chapped lips and puckering them at her. "Say, darling, can I kiss you?"

"No, sorry. You can't," Jo said, staring at the old man and

squeezing his hand so tight, she could break all his fingers. "Darling."

The old man pulled his hand back with a scowl, more shocked at Jo's audacity than the strength of her grip. He left Jo, muttering a few choice phrases as he moved to another table. Nothing Jo hadn't heard before. The whole cocktail table fell silent, as if it were a mortal sin for a woman to rebuke a man's advances. As if a woman should always allow an octogenarian groper to invade her body. As if women were prey to be pounced on and caught in trembling hands. Jo's ad stifled a laugh with a healthy gulp of champagne.

"I take it you don't know who that was."

"Oh, the grand master dinosaur?"

"Only the house speaker of the Congress. Good god, you are something, Joanna. I'm glad I'm with you tonight." He chuckled. "I'll have to pay for this in more ways than one. But whatever. Leaving old man Alvaro speechless is worth it."

The ad made the rounds again, leaving Jo to fend for herself. The bluish smoke made Jo's eyes water. With her fever, it was starting to get too warm for comfort. Sweat trickled down her nape and back. After a trip to the washroom, she decided to get some fresh air at the second-floor balcony.

"My, my. My eyes must be deceiving me." Jo gave a small jump at the sound of that voice. She looked over her shoulder and found the mistress leaning against the double doors. The mistress looked her up and down, and gave a low whistle of approval. "You look well."

"I didn't think I'd see you here."

"Feeling's mutual, dear." The mistress opened a silver cigarette case and offered it to Jo.

"Work?"

"Yes."

The mistress hissed, delighted by the prospect of gossip. "Do tell. Who are you with?"

Jo told her.

"I know him. A nice guy through and through. Not like any of these dumbfucks—did I use that word right? But, if he's your date, no sex tonight, then? That man has no time for anything else but his ships." The mistress ran a hand down Jo's bare back.

"How are you?"

Jo remembered the last time they saw each other. She remembered the bruised-up face, the gash on her lip, the labored throbbing of a heart so thoroughly destroyed by shattered hope. Jo wasn't quite healed from all of it yet; the mere recollection brought her stomach into knots.

"OK, I guess, all things considering. Been thinking of going away for some time. This city is so hard to love sometimes."

The mistress agreed with a short nod. "Taking a vacation?"

"A test drive, more like. If I like where I am, I might stay longer. Come back here for my stuff, then leave for good."

"Where are you off to?"

"Somewhere north. I'll take a bus to La Union, take another bus to Baguio, and another to some quiet town in the mountains, jump into a hole to the end of the world, all of the above," Jo said, with a nervous laugh and a shake of the head. "I don't know yet, to be honest."

"And Liza?"

Jo's gaze fell on the cars below. Red lights breezed by, people in transit, towards a destination, a desirable end. She was stuck here, in the city she once loved, this city she fucked and made love to, this city that took her under its wings and made a woman out of her, this city that mended her heart, only to break it again. A bitter smile formed on her lips; the mistress took that as an answer.

"You're not the only one rearranging a life around here," the mistress said, giving Jo's arm a poke, plucking her out of her reverie. "I'm not here with my husband, actually. I'm leaving him."

"For me?" Jo joked.

"Very funny," the mistress said, dismissing the notion with a wave of the hand and a short laugh. "The things I said to you back in the cottage? Finding happiness? I needed to hear them, too. I took some time alone, and boy, did it take a lot of time and strength to think it over."

She played with her cigarette case, clicking it open and shut to a steady one-two rhythm. "And, you know what, I'm done hosting his parties, making his bed, saying yes to all his decisions. I'm tired of him dangling this so-called good life at me, so I would be okay with being unhappy. As if misery is less of itself when you're driving a top-of-the-line car or sipping wine older than you."

Jo brushed her fingers across the mistress's wrist, across a faded tattoo that said "Live free" in cursive. There was a gleam of determination in the mistress's eye, a newfound will to take control, to be her own person. It was a look Jo had never seen in the years that she had known her.

"My lawyer's fighting for the cottage, though. If I win, will you come live with me?"

"Now, who's the clown?"

"In this dress? Certainly not me."

They both laughed, knowing full well that it was too little too late for dreams of a shared life. Their hearts were set on different paths, pulled towards different and uncharted territories. They did share the fear of starting over—that much was obvious. There was so much to lose, even in Jo's case. What would they do for money now? How would they survive with less? What kind of people would they meet along the way? That fear was there in the drumming of fingers on the steel railing. The bite marks of anxiety on a lower lip. The drawn-out sighs that spoke more of the untold future than any words ever could.

"Oh, if you're heading north, will you let me call a friend who runs a café in Sagada? Teresa should be able to take you in for a week or two, if you find yourself there."

"You don't have to do that."

"Consider it a parting gift."

Like old times, they had no rules on gifts in kind.

"I should be heading back."

The mistress gave Jo's hand a gentle tap, a reminder of their fondness, a wish of good fortune in the days ahead. Jo kissed her on the cheek, and left her to her teardrop earrings and half-smoked cigarettes.

Chapter 16

L iza's graveyard-shift roommates had shuffled out of the apartment. She meant to call Christopher, but decided on a few minutes of quiet, lying in bed and doing nothing. She allowed her mind to wander back to her old room in Laurel. She conjured the poster of the Backstreet Boys hanging on the wall. While enjoying a stick of Fortune she'd grifted from her father, Liza used to stare at that poster and imagined what it must be like being Mrs. Nick Carter. She played pretend until her mind grew tired and gave in to afternoon naps. She kept postcards from her friends in the U.S.: a red top-down convertible navigating a suspended bridge, with a flourish of "California Dreaming" over it; snow falling on the street while pedestrians huddled their coats closer; lovers sitting on the grass, bikes thrown by the wayside, not a care in the world. One day, she was going to be the one sending postcards like this.

All her best-laid plans were lined up, going smooth as could be. Everything except for this feeling in her gut, every single time she thought of Jo. Jo was nothing but a gut feel that lingered. It was a ride of emotions that Liza allowed to sweep her away. Jo was unpredictable and unsuitable, a con more than a pro. She did not fit Liza's plan, and it was the right decision to let her go. Liza had been telling herself these things since that night she left Jo's apartment and Jo's life for good. She'd managed to keep her distance. Not even one call or text to ask how Jo was. Whenever Jo crossed her mind, she would turn to the images of U.S. in her head. Fresh breeze, driving around in a car, Sundays lounging in the pool in Christopher's yard. Christopher was the plan. U.S. by way of Tampa Bay, Florida, was the destination.

Liza had never trusted gut feel. It made little sense to hinge the future on a split-second decision. Her life was a series of grand designs, of plotting the best possible outcome and preparing for the worst. Living in the U.S. was the best possible outcome. After nailing her visa interview, Liza was a one-way flight away from escaping this shitty rat race that nobody won anyway. There was no reason for this nagging pinch in her heart. There was no sense in entertaining this foreboding that something wasn't quite right.

"So, I'm choosing between the eighteenth and the twenty-fifth. Those look like the cheapest flights out of there," Christopher said, bringing Liza back to the present.

"And then, we need to get married within ninety days. Should go smoothly, no problem."

"The petitions for Nanay and Tatay might take a while. But we could get started once your papers are in order."

"I'll help you find a job, too, once your papers are—"

As Christopher went on and on about their future, Liza felt the harmless pinch in her heart grow into a pounding ache. It throbbed and coursed outwards, up to her head, down to her gut. That wretched gut feel was stronger this time. It persisted in pursuing Liza's attention. It planted ideas in her mind. Before she could stop it, gut feel had already forced the words out of her mouth.

"I can't marry you."

"Say that again?"

Liza could take the words back and blame it on the spotty connection. God knows it wouldn't be the first time Wi-Fi came between them. But when she opened her mouth to take it back, the same words came tumbling out. Her voice wore a boldness she didn't recognize.

"I can't marry you."

Christopher licked his lips slowly and peered closer to the screen. An amused smile crossed his face, upper lip twitching behind the full beard he now sported. Christopher thought this was a joke. What did he know to think otherwise?

"You're kidding, right, babe? I mean, everything is all set. The visa, the house, the papers."

"I don't want to marry you like this, Christopher," Liza said, tears already welling up in her eyes. Her voice did not waver, though. *Someday, I hope you realize that you matter, too.* She mattered. This was her life to live. She had a choice.

"What in hell are you talking about? What is going on?"

"I did love you, Christopher, and I wanted to be with you. But things happened. And, I'm so sorry I can't do this with you. I can't marry you out of guilt or obligation. I can't let you waste your life having a wife who doesn't think the world of you. You don't deserve that. I don't deserve that."

Christopher's reply was curt. "Who is it?"

"I swear, Christopher, I didn't expect this to happen."

"Who is it? Is it one of your exes? Is he on the site, too? Have you been entertaining other people this whole time? Tell me."

"It's Jo."

When she said the words, the heaviness inside her disappeared like magic. She allowed an unspeakable lightness, a sense of freedom, to curve her lips into a smile. Liza remembered the sureness of Jo's hand in hers, the trembling thrill of her kiss, the ice cream, the beer, and everything that followed suit. She might have lost Jo for good. It could be too late to heal what had been cut open. She would pay dearly for pushing Jo away, and could only hope to learn from it. But the ability to choose Jo now, to want her, to finally admit to this thrumming in her chest, was a bittersweet discovery in and of itself.

In her mind, she watched Nick Carter grow old and worn, his bright blue eyes turning into frosted glass, his hair falling into white tufts to mix with molten snow. She watched that red car from the postcard careen off a cliff. She watched the people in oversize coats disappear one by one, the light of lampposts snuffed street corner by street corner. Liza watched her dreams crumble, turn to soft mud, ready to be shaped again.

"You know what. Sleep on it. This is..." Christopher ruffled his hair and rubbed his temple with a tense hand. "Crazy and damned right fucked up is what it is. I don't know what's gotten into you, Liza. I don't even know you, and how you can say things like this. I can't accept it. I won't accept it. So, sleep on it. Get your shit together and talk to me tomorrow. For Christ's sake, I built a guest house for you. I want to marry you. I love you. Doesn't that mean anything?"

Then, he hung up.

Nothing changed the next morning. She didn't want to marry him anymore, and it didn't matter how many days he gave her to think it over.

Jo, really?

What were you thinking?

I lost to that—to that—Liza, how?

For weeks, they circled the same roundabout. Christopher

couldn't seem to accept that he'd lost to Jo, that all his grand gestures were for naught. He took his time wrapping his head around what had happened. Liza let Christopher process his grief. That grief soon morphed into denial. Denial fused with anger and bargaining, until the day he gave up and stopped calling. He kicked Liza off all his social media accounts. He deleted his profile in FlowerBrides and disappeared like a ghost, like the fourteenth. It was safe to say the engagement was off.

Now came the hard part: going home to Laurel.

"What do you mean, we're not going to America anymore?" Mang Carding's eyes almost bulged out of their sockets, jaw struggling against his hollow cheeks, lips pursed to a thin line. "Get back together with him, Liza. What were you even thinking? We were close! So close!"

"I can't, Papa. I'm sorry."

"What do you mean you can't?"

"I don't love him."

"What's love got to do with it? You think—you think love sends your brothers to school? Puts food on the table? You had a chance to make something of your life, Liza! You had the ticket to get us out of here, to America, like we always dreamed, and you blew it. All because of what? Love?" He spat that last word out like a bullet straight to Liza's chest. Blunt force, internal bleeding.

"You disappoint me," Mang Carding said, clicking his tongue before walking out.

"Carding!" was all her mother said, her voice caught between imploring and admonishing.

Alex watched from the kitchen doorway. Liza knew how he looked up to Christopher. When she'd told him that the petition was approved, it had been one of their more peaceful conversations of late. He'd asked how long until Liza could get them there, if he could work and make his own money there. This was a chance for Alex to steer the right course before it was too late—make something out of life, as Mang Carding said.

He glared at her like she'd just stolen his small collection of Jordans, scoffing and smirking in utter disbelief. He bit his lip and rubbed his nose. When they were kids, he'd done that to stop himself from crying. Right after Mang Carding left, he followed suit. He stormed out, mumbling, "What a joke," letting the shrill slam of the aluminum screen door spell out the rest of his reaction for him.

Liza had expected overrated and unfounded lament from Mang Carding. Alex played to the script, too, with his passive retreat out the back door. The aggressive would most likely come later. Mac was better off where he was, playing with friends by the lake, clueless to it all. It was her mother's silence that hit her the most. She sat beside Liza on the rattan sofa, watching Mang Carding and Alex walk out. Aling Luz's face was unmoved. Was it shock? Indifference? Liza couldn't read her mind, and her mother's face gave nothing away. Feeling like she had just been trampled on by a pack of horses, she withdrew to her room and stayed there until the church bells rang for Sunday Mass.

After the Mass, Liza attempted to broker a conversation with Aling Luz. She took her to their favorite noodle house. They needed to talk without Mang Carding hovering and clicking his tongue. They ate their lomi, Aling Luz taking her time with slurping the broth, Liza picking at the bits of egg on her bowl. On a normal day, she would have wolfed this down in five minutes flat. This was not a normal day. She didn't have the appetite for a good meal.

"What happened? I thought the petition was all OK."

Liza shifted her gaze to the throng of people going in and out of the church. Little children clung to their mothers. Old women with their scapulars and veils huddled around the grotto. Teenagers in their best clothes flocked the food booths.

"I fell for someone else, 'Nay. I went crazy for someone and it wasn't Christopher. And, if I married him, it would be for something else. Guilt, maybe. Comfort. Convenience? But, for sure, not love. I can't do that to him. I can't do that to myself." She finally had the courage to look her mother in the eye. "I made the right call, right, 'Nay? Or did I just throw my life, all our lives away?"

Aling Luz spoke slower than a turtle on a good day, milder than a priest absolving sins. But Liza knew better than to push that soft-heartedness to the limit. When provoked, her mother was not above a sermon. Liza braced for the disappointment and guilt that would wash over her soon enough. What she didn't expect was an apology, a hand reaching out from across the table. The rough lines on Aling Luz's palm were a comfort, telling Liza all she needed to know. It sure as hell didn't look like it now, but they would be okay.

"I'm sorry, anak."

"For what?"

"For letting you carry us on your shoulders all these years. I've always been thankful of how you helped us stay afloat. And I'm sorry for putting you in a situation where..." Aling Luz's voice cracked. She paused to clear her throat and drink some water. "...where you risked being miserable to make our lives better. I'm sorry for forcing you into that sacrifice."

Liza looked down and shaded her eyes. Her shoulders heaved up and down. She gave her eyes a good swipe and looked at her mother. Aling Luz was smiling, crooked dentures and all, tears streaming down her face. Like mother, like daughter.

"You are enough as you are."

"But, Alex and Papa... The things they said to me, the way they looked at me like I'm—"

"They will come around soon enough. Or maybe they won't. But I see you, Liza. I see all the good in you. You are more than enough, my child. More than enough, however you become."

Liza could care less if they were spoiling the lomi and letting it run cold. She could care less if people stopped to look at the two women causing a scene in a small noodle joint by the church. This was all that mattered to Liza right now. Holding her mother in her arms. Knowing and believing that she was loved, that she was and had always been more than enough.

They walked home, hands linked and swaying a little bit. Liza crossed the town plaza, licking a Popsicle before the heat beat her to it. She might as well have been six years old again. Only now, she was taller. It was Aling Luz leaning on her shoulder.

"It's Jo, isn't it?" Aling Luz asked.

"How did you know?"

"Nothing special. Gut feel," Aling Luz said, rubbing her tummy, a knowing smile playing at her lips. She gave Liza's arm a playful poke, before sobering up to ask the next question. "Does she love you?"

Liza paused and sighed, biting off the last of her Popsicle. She let it melt in her mouth. Jo was the master of casual encounters. She wanted. She desired. She lusted. Jo never loved anybody until Liza. It was a big deal for Jo. But what had Liza done? She'd thrown that love back in her face, as if she didn't want it.

"Yes, 'Nay. I think she did. But it's too late now, I guess."

"It's never too late to be happy, Liza. Never."

Friday night at the Appliance Center, Liza tried her best to enjoy the party that wasn't for her anymore. The going-away theme was scratched last minute when Liza told them that she'd called off the engagement, but they insisted on throwing it anyway. It was a shame to waste all the work. Stricter security made these after-work gatherings quite a rarity. So she tried to take her mind off things and have a good time. Friends surrounded her like a shield, with various reasons for chatting her up. The ones she held dear, like Randy and Mara, knew not to push the issue. They knew Liza would talk when she was ready. Others offered their sympathy. There were a few who gave their sharpest click of the tongue at what they perceived a lost opportunity. A golden egg dropped and wasted. She was sure of the news now. Liza Dimaandal, the almost-U.S. citizen who turned down a sure-shot ticket to America. She would be trending for days and weeks to come.

After recounting the breakup a million times, Liza popped open a beer and retreated to a corner. This was the same corner where she'd almost kissed Jo. She drew out a strawberry ChapStick from her pocket, lathering her lips until they were as sticky as glue. "Piano in the Dark" was playing on the karaoke. The first song she had ever heard Jo sing. A desperate longing filled her chest close to bursting. Randy sat beside her and offered her a plate of assorted chips. Out of politeness, Liza picked at some of the cheese curls.

"Isn't Jo coming at all?" Randy asked.

"Why? Did you invite her? Did you talk to her?"

"Whoa, slow down there, ex-bride to be." Randy raised a hand between them. "We met at the department store last week. Told me she couldn't come because she's leaving Manila."

Randy looked at his plastic calculator watch. "What I remember is she's leaving in a few hours."

"For good?"

"Looks like she'll be gone a while."

"Did she say where?"

Randy shrugged, unable to supply an answer. "She told me you guys had a falling out? The hell was that about? You two were as tight as my ex's ass."

"Does she know the engagement's off?"

"I told her, yeah. Shouldn't I have?"

Liza slumped further in her corner, mind emptied of any other thought. Her heart dropped to her stomach like an anchor, legs without the strength to keep her upright. What she wouldn't do to see Jo one more time before she left. Would Jo want to see her, though? Would Jo at least let her say goodbye? Forgiveness was a 50-50 chance. Or 10-90, if Liza were to shed her optimism. But no matter how Jo felt about her, she would give an arm and a leg to see her one last time. Liza would spin a thousand times around that Ferris wheel until she puked all her insides out. She would leap a million times over the falls. She would give it all up to hold Jo's hand again, to kiss her again, to hear her sing again.

Liza chugged down her beer. The warm courage slid down her throat and spread like blood to her veins. Her mother said it was never too late to be happy. Her mother said these stirrings in her stomach were more reliable than reason. Gut feel. If that were true, there was only one way to find out. She ditched her own ex-engagement party to see Jo one last time.

"Fuck it. Fuck, fuck, fuck, fuck," Liza muttered to herself, frisking her pockets as she turned the corner towards the main street. In her hurry, she'd forgotten her wallet. And phone. And bag. What was she to do? Walk all the way to Ermita? It was as if the universe was conspiring against her, milking the clock, making sure she didn't get to Jo in time. Was this her punishment, some sort of ill-timed karma? She refused the idea. Not tonight. No, not tonight.

She ran back to the Appliance Center, her legs aching in protest at the bursting sprint. Her breath hitched out a gasp at the sight of a familiar figure standing outside the door grills. The figure kept shifting her weight from one foot to another, seemingly unsure about going inside. Although Liza would recognize that breadth of unkempt, wavy hair from anywhere, the gray crop top was a dead giveaway.

Chapter 17

I t was as if the universe were telling Jo not to go. Well, it could talk all it wanted, play hide-and-seek with her favorite shirts, send a couple of thousand-peso bills missing, rip the last good traveling bag she had. There was no stopping Jo from taking this trip. She felt the itch in her feet, the tense anticipation coursing through her body, the balloon of energy keeping her from being still. No, there was no stopping her now. But maybe, she conceded, she needed a new heavy-duty, universe-proof backpack first.

After a couple of hours scouring the department store, Jo scored the heavy-duty, universe-proof backpack at a 50 percent discount. She was strolling along, choosing between egg noodles and chicken wings for lunch, when she bumped into Randy. He had shaved his head and lost some weight. She almost didn't recognize him.

"Jo! Jo, isn't it? Liza's friend? How's it been?" Randy said with a tentative tap on Jo's shoulder.

"Randy? Did I remember that right?" She shook his hand. "I'm good, I'm good. Leaving Manila pretty soon."

"Oh? Abroad?"

"No. Just... around."

"But you will make it to Liza's going-away—oh wait, it's just a party now, I forgot."

Jo's breath hitched. Her mouth went dry. She gulped down the lump in her throat. What did he mean by *just a party now*? She fidgeted with the strap of her new backpack, as she tried to make sense of what Randy had just said.

"What do you mean?"

"The engagement is off now. Didn't she tell you?"

"Why did they break up?"

"She wouldn't say. But you know how it is with that friend of ours. Dumped, ghosted, traded for a cheaper, younger wife. Take your pick," Randy said with a shrug.

"When's the party?"

"Friday next week." Jo would be leaving that same week, Saturday morning. All the things she wouldn't take to the trip were stowed in boxes, stacked neatly in a corner of her closet. For the next three months, she would be on the road, taking on odd jobs like before, shuttling from one transient inn to another. After that, who knows? Maybe she'd come back. Maybe she won't. What she did know was that she didn't want to plunge herself back into this Liza-centric prison that she'd taken months to escape from. Going to the party and seeing her would do just that. She was a week away from riding a bus out of here, from a clean break, from a new lease on life. She did not need emotional baggage as an excess carry-on.

Randy reached for Jo's hand and gave it a squeeze. "Come on. Eat and then run if you like. Whatever happened between you two, forget about it. I'm sure Liza would be happy to see you."

Jo didn't think much of the party until she found herself sprawled in bed that Friday night. She'd just got home from another girlfriend experience ad. She shouldn't have taken it, but she couldn't resist a gracious, one-for-the-road exit. The ad thought it was romantic walking about in an open-space art museum in the sweltering heat. Jo's feet throbbed at the slightest pressure. Her skin was hot to the touch. This tight pencil-cut dress made her sweat like a pig. All she wanted was to lie down on her bare bed and nap for a couple of hours.

Tonight was Liza's not-going-away party. It tugged at Jo's mind like a stubborn snag that demanded to be pulled. Leave it. Chuck the memory of Liza in the deepest recesses of her mind. Reduce her to a passing blip on the radar.

Did she want to be wiped clean of Liza?

Did she want to forget?

Did Liza deserve it?

Jo grabbed a gray crop top and skinny jeans from a box. She fished for a pair of socks and massaged her feet before easing them into her favorite leather boots. The tiny voice had won. She would go there and say goodbye, good luck, see you never, whatever people say to ex-friends who became the love of their lives, who then chose to ruin them so completely that they had to leave the city they'd called home for five years. All there was to it. What harm could it possibly do?

She reached the Appliance Center and found the grills partially closed. Only a cat could slip into that small of an opening. Yellow light bled into the sidewalk and at her feet. Jo could hear an off-key and quite drunken rendition of "Love Will Lead You Back." The chorus was butchered into pieces. Even Taylor Dayne herself wouldn't recognize it. She imagined Liza cradling a sweaty bottle of beer, laughing along.

Jo had thought she was ready for this. The dark days were over. The heartbreak had played itself out. She had paid for it with countless bottles of beer and sobbing monologues. In the end, as her friend, Jo understood why Liza did it. Survival. The prospect of a better life. Putting family first. People made that choice every single day, and Liza was no different. Jo should be okay with this. But now faced with the event of seeing Liza after all these months, Jo didn't know what to do. She couldn't even take a step, as light and shadow continued to play at her feet. Her heart was telling her to go inside. Her mind was trying to convince her that there was nothing, absolutely nothing, to see here.

She closed her eyes and sighed. Her mind was right. Show's over, nothing to say goodbye to but dashed hopes and snuffed dreams. It was time to move along.

Chapter 18

"Looking for somebody?"

Jo turned around to see Liza, waving a weak hello, an even weaker smile on her face. They stood on opposite ends of the narrow sidewalk, neither wanting to say the first word.

"I left him."

"I'm leaving."

They ended up saying it at the same time, their realities colliding in so short an exchange. It was yet to be seen if this collision would break them apart, never to intersect again, or keep them together. Was this the tangent, the origin, or the destination? Jo shut her eyes and nodded, waiting for Liza to speak.

There was no time to be fancy, for rehearsed speeches bordering on poetry, for a memorable movie reference. When Liza opened her mouth, there was only space for the truth. Blunt. Unadorned. Unable to stop, not even for a breath or a well-timed pause, until it reached its end.

"I left him. We were talking about flights out of here, and the plans kept pouring out of his mouth. Get married as soon as I arrive, work on the petition in the next three years to get Nanay and everyone with us. It was happening. It was happening. All the things I have imagined for the last ten years, they're finally coming true. And I meant to say 'I love you,' but what came out was 'I can't marry you.' He asked me if I was joking, and I wanted to say yes. How easy! How convenient! But, then, the words came to me again, like I've wanted to say them for a long time. 'I can't marry you.' And he asked who it is. Is it some ex-boyfriend on the site? Then I told him it was you. I told him every day until he stopped calling that it was..."

Liza dared to close the distance between them, taking a step from the lamppost.

Jo hung on to every word, but still gave her nothing to stand on. She was content to put Liza in this one-foot-in, one-foot-out limbo.

"It still is you."

She reached for Jo, who flinched and drew two steps back. Liza's hand trembled, suspended in mid-air, before falling limply back to her side.

"I have to go, Liza, not only because my trip's in three hours," Jo said with a shake of the head. "I need to do this for myself. Watching you leave broke me. You know how big a deal that was for me? Nobody's ever stayed, and I had been fine with that. I've built a life around leaving, told stories around goodbyes. The first time, Liza, the first fucking time I wanted someone to stay..."

Jo's voice trailed off, the weight of her body falling against a nearby wall. The dark months had balled up somewhere inside her, rising, exacting their revenge. She braced herself, embraced herself for the hurt. She should have kept silent—the damage would have been much less. But she had kept this in for too long. Her mouth had forgone the Stop button.

"You knew how much it took to get there. To want you. To

finally admit to myself that I love someone. That I love you. But you made me pay for it. You made me feel like I wasn't good enough or big enough. Wasn't enough, period."

Liza looked up at the orange glow of the lamppost, before placing both hands on her head, face hidden behind her arms. Jo knew this look—it was Liza at a loss. Her speech had not worked to plan. Her speech did not unsay the words or undo the decisions. It did little to erase the hurt she caused Jo.

"I'm leaving."

"I know." Liza sighed, defeated.

"Goodbye, Liza."

Jo heard a whimper in response.

Every step towards home magnified the hollow silence inside Jo. It was hardly a quiet night. The city of neon and concrete and chrome never skips a beat. But all this noise did not compare to the pounding in her ears, the rhythm telling her to go back, Liza's whimper playing repeatedly in her head. She dared not turn back to check. But with every step, she could feel Liza's eyes watching her.

Just turn the corner, Jo.

A car honked past.

Five more steps.

Footsteps of strangers clacked against the cheap concrete.

Time to close this.

Somewhere, there was the shrill noise of stores locking up.

One more step. Disappear.

She stopped right under the street sign. Coral Way corner Seaside Drive. If her life turned to shit, Jo would have this street corner to blame. This ocean-themed street corner would be her ruin. Or, perhaps, there was a chance it would spell her happiness, at last. She was supposed to turn right and disappear.

She wasn't supposed to do a 180 and walk back to the lamppost where Liza still stood.

"I'm leaving," Jo said, slightly out of breath.

"You said that already, yes—"

Jo pulled Liza into her arms and brushed her cheek against hers. They both felt the tug of the thread that bound them—a sliver of hope for that life together. The thread once seemed unbreakable; now, it was fragile and frayed. One wrong pull could break them apart for good.

"But I want to give this a try. And that starts with being by myself for a while."

Jo looked at Liza's eyes, and knew that she understood. *This won't solve itself overnight; it will take time. This won't be a walk along the breakwater, balancing a Coke and a shawarma in both hands. Trying to carve a life together will be exhausting and frustrating. The past will rear its ugly head, seemingly at will. Scars will threaten to become fresh again. The only way to go through it is to face the pain, the wounds that hadn't healed. Go through it.*

Liza gave a short nod and a small smile.

"Will you come back, then?"

Instead of answering, Jo kissed Liza with all the hope in her broken heart. She kissed her like there was a new beginning to look forward to. She imagined kissing her every night like this until the years had shown on her face. Until her strongest days were behind her. Until her heart could beat no more. Jo meant to grow and be whole again. The cold mountain air, the fresh marketplace fare, the slow hum of time by an obscure beach would be the good earth to plant a new life in. Jo walked away for the second time, finally turning the corner. She was soon out of Liza's sight, but hoping against hope that she wouldn't be out of Liza's mind.

Epilogue

The first stop out of Manila was La Union. Elyu. That small pocket of sand and surf that inspired box-office movies and new beginnings. It reminded Jo of her birthplace; it struck her how much she missed being near the sea. The never-ending ebb and flow of wide-eyed first-timers and suntanned been-there-done-that veterans gave La Union its pulse. Jo felt it the moment she settled into a capsule room in the form of a hippie Volkswagen bus. This was going to be her home for the next two weeks. Anything longer than that was beyond Jo's foresight. For the first three days, she took in the salt, the sharp smell of fish and moss and clean air, the sand beneath her feet. She hustled for a cheap rash guard and charmed her way into a discounted surf class.

Imagine her surprise when she showed up to her first lesson and found Van Tomas, only her most favorite member of her most favorite girl band, leading the class. She had to blink four times and crab-pinch the flesh on her waist to convince herself that she wasn't hallucinating. Van Tomas, of Weekend Club fame, was her instructor. If the tabloids were to be believed, Jo knew why Van Tomas was holed up here six hours away from Manila and its rave parties and never-ending hustle. Still, it was strange being in the same space with someone she had only ever seen on TV.

"Can I get your autograph?" Jo blurted out, the cool-cat hello she'd planned lost in translation. She was out of breath, tired and bloated from swallowing a fuckton of saltwater. Former child of the water as she was, she'd found out that surfing wasn't as easy as it looked.

"Uhm?"

"I mean, hi again. I'm Jo, in case you're not very good with names."

"Hi, Jo!" Van said. "Listen, I'm about to grab dinner. Do you want to come along?"

Was she ready for this? Pre-heartbreak Jo would have killed this. Spilling with confidence, she would have charmed the socks off Van Tomas, right at the first hello. Post-heartbreak Jo couldn't even say hi. Post-heartbreak Jo was deathly afraid of rejection. Post-heartbreak Jo was—wait, this wasn't about keeping things as they were. This was supposed to be a reclamation of parts she lost, parts she had to pull out to be able to survive Liza's leaving, parts she had to forget in an effort to not feel anything.

So in this little vegan, no-alcohol stall, she urged herself to say the right words. Bring a little bit of that swagger back. Truth was, the past didn't matter as much as here and now. And the Jo here and now wanted to go home with Van Tomas.

"Do you want to get out of here?" Jo went for it.

"God, yes." Van said, surprising Jo a bit.

They went to Van's because two people were a crowd in a converted Volkswagen bus with a single bed and a low ceiling. It was also convenient that Van's roommate-slash-sober-companion was on three-day retreat to a farm in Pangasinan. They had sex for a few rounds, before settling into pillow talk.

Jo picked up the guitar on the wall and started to play.

"You sing?"

"Used to. In a KTV bar."

"No shit?"

"I tried those TV auditions once upon a time. Didn't work."

"There's gonna be a new season, I heard."

"Do you ever see yourself going back?" Jo asked.

"No."

"Why not?"

"What for? I'm far from everything that has made my life hell. Except—"

"Except what?"

Van shook her head before sitting up on the edge of the bed. "It doesn't matter. It would take the world to uproot me from here." She snatched the guitar from Jo and absently strummed on the strings. Jo picked up the melody. It was "Come Closer" by Weekend Club. Co-written with Ali Andrade, if Jo got her fangirl facts right. She saw the dull regret in Van's eyes, and decided against singing along.

***

Once her lease was up, Jo packed her things and rode towards Baguio. Having gotten her confidence and a semblance of her top-grade social skills, she talked her way into a two-day group tour and a decent room share.

All the strawberries reminded her of Liza. That battered strawberry ChapStick she carried around. Carving a hole in the three-in-one ice cream tub, scraping all the strawberry and leaving out the chocolate and cheese. That sickly sweet strawberry cologne she insisted on wearing. *Now is not the time.* She shook the thoughts out of her head. Far be it from Liza, even virtual representations of her, not to be stubborn as fuck.

142

The last straw was coffee and cake at a café along Session Road. The strawberry shortcake was divine. There was no other word to describe it. A gelatin of fresh strawberries on a generously frosted sponge cake. Riding the foodgasm high, Jo thought it as good a time as any to finally break the radio silence. This was ridiculous; they'd kissed before she left, and she promised to try. But so far, there were zero kisses and the exact opposite of trying.

After a short stint at an adjacent bar, she excused herself from the group, and walked to the transient inn by herself. She snatched a can of beer from the fridge, and walked towards the small balcony. Jo stared at her phone, her free hand drawing circles around her forehead and eyes and mouth. She puffed out a small smoke of air before pressing Liza's name. Jo meant to switch it to a faceless call, no video, but Liza answered before she could.

"Hi," Liza said, hair all messy, eyes bleary and a little red.

Jo said the first thing that was on her mind, which oddly wasn't "Hello, how are you?" like a normal person who was trying to break the ice and be friends with an ex again. Almost-ex. Never-ex. Labels were such a hassle sometimes.

"I had sex with Van Tomas," was the first thing on Jo's mind. She cringed.

"Is that supposed to mean anything?" Liza replied with a yawn, confusion forcing creases on her forehead.

"Van Tomas is—"

"I know who Van Tomas is. I'm more of an Ali Andrade kind of girl. But whatever. Did you really call me at..." Liza sat up and looked at the wall clock behind her, before giving her cheeks a good wake-up slap. "...eleven p.m. just to say that?"

"I miss you. All the fucking strawberries here are making me miss you."

Liza gave a restrained smile, one that tried its hardest to tamp down the hope trying to spill out of her. She covered her mouth with her left hand. When she removed it, the smile was still there, but smaller. "Does this mean you're coming back?"

Jo shook her head. "No. Not there yet."

"Are you ever?"

"Ever what?"

"Coming back?"

When Jo responded with a painful silence, the small smile on Liza's face curved into a frown. "What does this mean, then? You calling me and saying you had a one-night stand with a celebrity, and that you miss me?"

"I don't know."

"Try, Jo, try."

"I—I guess I want us to be friends again."

A bigger smile, this time. No restraint. "Does this mean, at least, that I can call you? Ask how you are? Share a Red Horse and Double Dutch with you on video call?"

"I'd love that. Good night. Sorry for waking you."

"Well, good night. I hope you're well. I l—" Liza paused. "I miss you, too."

Jo felt a part of her locking back into place, squeezing into the void, filling her heart with a strange feeling of hope. It was true that she wasn't ready to go back just yet. There was a chance she wouldn't go back ever, period, full stop. But calling Liza made Jo feel less uncertain about it. She smiled at her dead phone, and looked out into the well-lit Baguio night, looking forward to listening to Liza's non-stop stories about work gossip and Nanay and her brothers. And, maybe bit by bit, they could start talking about *them* again.

Like old times, like old times, but all so new.

***

Being this up north was a new thing to Jo. Good thing her roommates in Baguio were taking their trip to Sagada, too; she wouldn't have to endure the journey alone. They'd be traveling further north, and asked if Jo wanted to come.

"No, thanks. I'll stick to Sagada for now. See you around, then!" Jo said, bidding them farewell at the bus station, as she walked towards the address the mistress had given her.

The mistress's connection came through and offered her a cashier job at a little cafe that served the best lemon pie in town. On Friday nights, for a little bit extra money, she took the stage for a five-song set before closing. Nothing to write home about. Just a few songs on the guitar to see the last patrons home. It felt right singing again. Her life felt right, felt like her own again, felt like herself again. Like the taste of the salty air in La Union, she didn't realize how much she'd missed this part of her.

As promised, Liza called more often, usually at night when they'd both settle themselves to sleep after a day at work.

"You make me want to go there," Liza said, ogling at the lemon pie Jo had brought home. "That looks delicious."

"Me or the pie?"

"The pie. And it's not even close."

"Wow, Liza. Way to make a girl feel special."

Jo was about to keep the banter going, when a TV commercial caught her eye. It was the show that did her in, the last audition Jo ever took before she shelved her pop star plans for good. It was also the show that launched the careers of her favorites: Lonely Monkeys, Janna Ramirez, Weekend Club.

New season, like Van Tomas said. They even had new judges and a new format. The universe was offering Jo another crack at it. One thing, though. She'd have to come back to Manila for the audition. This meant seeing Liza again, the idea striking her with anticipation and dread. They were doing so well apart, the physical distance remedied by daily doses of video calls. She didn't know what would happen if they were in the same city again. Was she ready for her, for the audition, for all of it to start anew? Was she whole again, whole and brave enough to face heartbreak if it came?

As she was wont to do when she needed to distract herself, she devoted her hours to work. She pitched to sing on Wednesday nights as well. She volunteered to help in Teresa's organic garden at the back of the café. On weekends, she went spelunking, or trekked down to the waterfalls for a cold swim. She did everything she could to fill the hours with work and noise. But in the quiet and idle hours, when she would sometimes wake up at three a.m., her brain would circle back to the idea and deprive her of sleep.

It was another Friday night. She felt like extending her set to accommodate requests. Jo received one from a middle-aged woman who was celebrating her birthday. Jo unfolded the piece of tissue and gave a low whistle. Well, if this wasn't a sign, the universe was losing its cryptic touch. "Piano In The Dark," it said in blotchy blue ink and scraggly handwriting. With a smile, she pocketed the 100-peso bill that came with the request. She closed her eyes, picturing Liza in the crowd. She dared to imagine the audition judges, a jam-packed stadium, two packs of shawarma after a concert. She got so lost in her dreams that she missed the opening riff.

"Hey," her guitarist whispered, nudging her arm lightly.

"Sorry. Sorry. I was inside my head for a bit." Jo threw a peace sign at the customer who asked for the song. "Let's give that another go. Here's for your birthday."

Every verse was a step towards a decision. Jo realized that she was never going to be ready for all the uncertainties; life is a fickle thing, anyway. She only had to be brave to say yes. By the end of the last chorus, as the guitars faded to a soft strumming, Jo knew what she wanted to do. She excused herself, and asked for a bathroom break. Seeing that Liza was online, Jo typed the words and sent them before a wave of fear could change her mind. They could iron things out later, but it was important that she say this now.

I'm coming back. For an audition. For you.

Jo watched the three dots dance on the screen anxiously, waiting for Liza's reply.

I'll be here. For the audition.

Dancing dots.

For you.

Dancing dots. Longer, this time. Either Liza was churning out a five-page message or backspacing the hell out of the keyboard.

For all of it.

And, just in case Jo wondered if it was indeed Liza on the other end, another message followed right after.

Took you damn long enough, Joanna haha
Wait a little longer?
Better have five boxes of lemon pie with you, then.

***

Another three weeks passed before Jo settled things and boarded the morning bus back to Manila. It was a long ride, but she couldn't sleep. The seats were uncomfortable. The man beside her smelled like gin and sardines. More than these discomforts, the giddiness in her heart kept her awake. What would she sing at the auditions? She thought of Van in La Union.

Maybe some of those slow songs in the underrated *Mirrors* album. What if it ended like all the others? She looked at her phone. No text from Liza. Not even a missed call. Would she even be there when Jo got to her apartment?

Balintawak exit. She was a good hour away from Manila. The roads were uncharacteristically bare; where was that patent calibrated-for-mental-torture time-wasting Manila traffic when you needed to buy time? She needed time to think. Time to compose herself. Time to quiet down the constant flutter in her chest. She could swear her heart was somewhere behind her right lung now.

She slowed down as she walked her way back to the apartment complex. The landlady saw her coming and passed her the key to the apartment.

"Welcome back. Your friend's been waiting for you all day."

Jo gulped as she turned towards the stairway, all sweaty and breathless from carrying all her luggage up the stairs. She saw Liza, holding a bunch of flowers in one hand, half a cigarette in the other. Her highlights were as faded and badly done as Jo remembered. It only took a shuffle against the weathered floor tiles for Liza to glance in Jo's general direction.

"Where have you been? What took you so long?"

God, she missed that voice. The way it grated when Liza got impatient or waited too long. Jo slowed her step just to piss her off a little bit, eliciting a short huff from Liza. Jo stood in front of her, and moved all her luggage to the side of the door, not saying anything. She would deal with these later.

"I've been waiting—"

Jo kissed her, like she had dreamed of during one too many cold nights in Sagada, before she could say anything more. Truth was, they had both been waiting, wanting, longing to arrive to this moment. Jo took in the smell of Liza's hair, welcomed the warm blush when their skins touched. No, she still wasn't one to cry. But the lump in her throat was close enough. The explanations had to wait a little longer. She thought she would have no reason to go back. She thought her life would set sail and anchor somewhere else. But with the way her heart was cracking open right now, she knew that there was nowhere she'd rather be than here in the grainy, dirty glow of a lightbulb, staring at the woman who gave meaning to it all.

"Hey...," Liza said.

"You have no idea where I've been."

"Tell me, then."

"It can wait."

There was a witty comeback lingering in Jo's brain, about déjà vu. About coming full circle. She wanted to share her plans for the audition. She wanted to recount her travels—the surfing, the hidden spots in Baguio, her brush with fame, her dreams resurrected. But she let all that go and instead held Liza in her arms. For now, this was the most important thing. She was ready. She was all in. She was home, at last.

END

Acknowledgements

This story went through a lot of stops and starts, and more revisions than I bothered to count. Thanks to everyone who helped me finally get this out into the universe.

Dani: for slapping a bangin' cover on this little story; for being patient on explaining to me what bleeds and spines are.

Mary, Agay and Arki Caryn : for agreeing to beta-read You, Me, U.S. and steering my first draft to the right course.

Ron : for catching my abrupt segues (hahaha my sickness) and helping me write more smoothly; for flagging weird scenes and out-of-character dialogue.

Rica: for the technical read-through and a couple of grammar lessons that I would definitely carry to the next manuscript.

Mina, and the whole romanceclass community: for providing me with the daily inspiration to keep writing; for all the workshops and sessions that helped me create this thing; this community is so awesome, and I'm just so happy I get to hang and chat and learn with you online and in real life. More books, please, always and forever, thank you.

Oya: for bearing the heavy brunt of my rants and complaints, whenever I got a bad case of writer's block; for talking me through the difficult things, not only in writing this story but also in figuring out this life.

Jeter and Blanchett (they're people-ish, fight me) : for stepping on my laptop; for keeping me company; for providing the daily comic relief.

And, to you, dear reader, for taking a chance on Jo and Liza.

About The Author

Hello! I'm Brigitte Bautista, and I'm currently juggling my day job as a software engineer and my passion for writing. I was a participant in Anvil's very own #SparkNA writing workshop, where my first novel "Don't Tell My Mother" was produced. Since then, the novel has been included in National Bookstore's best-selling list. More recently, I have worked with #romanceclass as co-editor and contributor of Start Here, a romance anthology of m/m, f/f and nonbinary/f stories.

Also by Brigitte Bautista

Don't Tell My Mother

With an overly zealous mother as her guide, 19-year-old Sam has never had problems navigating through Christian suburbia before. But, all that changes when she befriends and becomes intrigued with Clara, her widowed neighbor and the village's social outcast. When their friendship grows into the "unnatural", Sam is forced to examine her upbringing and come to terms with who she really is.

Buy on Amazon Kindle

Start Here : Short Stories of First Encounters

There's a first time for everything. Gatecrashing a KPop concert with an oppa in a business suit. Taking shelter from the storm with the girl you've been meaning to shake off. That kiss that blurs the line between friendship and something more. A one-night stand (or, is it?) with your best friend from across the hallway.

Dive into these 10 stories of first encounters – unapologetically queer, happy endings required, with a smattering of that signature #romanceclass kilig. Whether you're recalling your own firsts or out there looking for one, there's a story in here for you.

Buy on Amazon Kindle

Editors : Ronald S. Lim and Brigitte Bautista

Authors: Brigitte Bautista, Motzie Dapul, Agay Llanera, H. Bentham , Ella Banta , Danice Sison , Yeyet Soriano , Barbie Barbieto, Katt Briones

Made in United States
North Haven, CT
12 January 2024